P9-CJL-113

NO LONGER PROPERTY OF
SEATTLE PUBLIC LIBRARY

MEET ME
HALFWAY

ALSO BY ANIKA FAJARDO

What If a Fish

MEET ME HALFWAY

ANIKA FAJARDO

Simon & Schuster Books for Young Readers
NEW YORK   LONDON   TORONTO   SYDNEY   NEW DELHI

SIMON & SCHUSTER BOOKS FOR YOUNG READERS
An imprint of Simon & Schuster Children's Publishing Division
1230 Avenue of the Americas, New York, New York 10020

This book is a work of fiction. Any references to historical events, real people, or real places are used fictitiously. Other names, characters, places, and events are products of the author's imagination, and any resemblance to actual events or places or persons, living or dead, is entirely coincidental.

Text © 2022 by Anika Fajardo
Jacket illustration © 2022 by E.J. Chong
Jacket design by Sarah Creech © 2022 by Simon & Schuster, Inc.
All rights reserved, including the right of reproduction in whole or in part in any form.

SIMON & SCHUSTER BOOKS FOR YOUNG READERS
and related marks are trademarks of Simon & Schuster, Inc.
For information about special discounts for bulk purchases, please contact Simon & Schuster Special Sales at 1-866-506-1949 or business@simonandschuster.com.
The Simon & Schuster Speakers Bureau can bring authors to your live event. For more information or to book an event, contact the Simon & Schuster Speakers Bureau at 1-866-248-3049 or visit our website at www.simonspeakers.com.
Interior design by Hilary Zarycky
The text for this book was set in Adobe Garamond Pro.
The illustrations for this book were rendered in Adobe Garamond Pro.
Manufactured in China
0522 SCP
First Edition
2 4 6 8 10 9 7 5 3 1

Library of Congress Cataloging-in-Publication Data
Names: Fajardo, Anika, author.
Title: Meet me halfway / Anika Fajardo.
Description: First edition. | New York : Simon & Schuster Books for Young Readers, [2022] | Audience: Ages 8–12. | Audience: Grades 4–6. |
Summary: When seventh-grade classmates Mattie Gómez and Mercedes Miller realize they have the same Colombian father, they hatch a plan to run away from a school field trip to meet him for the first time.
Identifiers: LCCN 2022002246 |
ISBN 9781534495906 (hardcover) | ISBN 9781534495920 (ebook)
Subjects: CYAC: Families—Fiction. | Colombian Americans—Fiction. | Racially mixed people—Fiction. | Middle schools—Fiction. | Schools—Fiction. | LCGFT: Novels.
Classification: LCC PZ7.1.F3475 Me 2022 | DDC [Fic]—dc23
LC record available at https://lccn.loc.gov/2022002246

To my mom

CHAPTER 1

Mattie

B rown eyes flecked with amber peer back at me. Above them are my eyebrows, a little bushier than usual. There's my smallish nose, the one my mom says I inherited from my father. I turn my head, tilt my chin. But the face I'm studying doesn't move.

"What are you looking at?" the girl demands.

"Nothing," I mumble, embarrassed for getting caught staring at her. But I can't stop. Back home, at the Minnesota State Fair, there's a funhouse with a hall of mirrors, each one distorted to make you taller or fatter, shorter or skinnier. In those mirrors, you can see yourself, only different. Looking at the face across from me, I feel like I'm in that funhouse instead of a seventh-grade classroom.

The girl is wearing jean shorts and a T-shirt that says *Throw like a girl*. Her hair is the same brown as mine, although hers is smooth and loose around her shoulders, while I always wear my curls in a tight ponytail. She's looking everywhere but at me.

"Boys and girls," announces the social studies teacher. The chaos of the first-period classroom quiets. "We have a new student today."

It's not the first day of school for Poppy View Middle School, but it's *my* first day. I slouch in my seat, wishing I could disappear.

"Would you please introduce yourself," the teacher says, gesturing for me to join her at the front of the room.

My stomach tightens. I slink out of my chair and avoid making eye contact. I hate being in the spotlight, so I'm relieved that only a few students seem to care who I am. Most are doodling in their notebooks or checking their phones in their laps.

"Um, hi." I shift from one foot to the other.

And that's when, one by one, all the kids in my new class—except the girl in the seat across from mine—turn to stare. They switch off their phones. They put down their pencils. They lean toward each other, whispering. They nod and point. At me. My palms get sweaty. My toes curl in embarrassment.

"I'm Mattie," I croak. What did I do wrong? Did they want my whole story? Was I supposed to give my full name? "Gómez," I add a little uncertainly. I'm the only Gómez in my family now. When my mom got remarried over Labor Day weekend, she took Bob's last name—Jasper—dropping Gómez like it didn't mean anything, like there wasn't a whole story behind it.

"Welcome, Mattie. Now, I want everyone to—"

The teacher is interrupted by a boy whose hair sticks up in a spike at the back of his head. "Mrs. Ellingham," he calls out, "why does the new girl look just like Mercedes Miller?"

There are more murmurs. Mrs. Ellingham looks at me. She looks at the girl seated across from my desk. "Mercedes and Mattie do look very similar," she agrees.

The girl who must be Mercedes Miller is studying her mint-green fingernails like they're the most interesting thing in the world.

Mrs. Ellingham looks at us like we're a puzzle. She nods her head of gray hair. She's tall and looks even taller in the long, billowy dress she's wearing. "Maybe they're related," she suggests.

Related? I've never seen this girl before in my life. But there's a strange twitch in the back of my brain, even as I think this. And, although warm California sun is streaming through the classroom windows, a shiver thrums from my toes to my fingertips. I can't tell if it's one of my panic attacks or something else.

Mrs. Ellingham's bright-pink lipstick creases as she smiles. "*Are* you two related?"

"No," we say. Even though we speak in unison, our voices are different. Mine is small and just a little squeaky. Hers is bold, forceful, as if the idea of being related to me is the worst thing in the world.

"Well," says Mrs. Ellingham, looking from me to Mercedes. "I'm sure you two will end up being great friends." She smiles again.

She's the only one smiling.

"In the meantime, let's get to today's lesson."

I scurry back to my seat and resume my spot across from Mercedes. She seems to be pretending that I don't exist, which is a lot like what everyone has been doing around me lately. My new stepbrothers act like I'm a piece of the furniture, Bob follows my mom around like a lovesick puppy, and my mom juggles the three of them while unpacking and reorganizing our stuff at the new house.

"We're starting our mythology project today," Mrs. Ellingham says. She writes the word "mythology" on the whiteboard in swirling letters. "The mythology of a culture reveals that culture's history and beliefs." She underlines "mythology" with a flourish. Below it, she writes: "Greek," "Roman," "Maya," "Inca," "Egyptian." "Studying the stories of ancient civilizations helps us understand our own lives."

I think about my new life here in California. I'm pretty sure ancient civilizations aren't going to help me understand any of this.

"Hey!" I hear a hoarse whisper behind me as Mrs. Ellingham continues to talk about myths. "Hey, Mercedes and new girl."

I turn around to see the boy with the spiky hair leaning back in his chair. He whispers, "You guys are probably doppelgängers."

"Doppel-what?" I whisper back.

Mercedes glares at me and the boy.

"A doppelgänger. You know, someone who looks just like you. Like twins only not."

Twins? I examine Mercedes. She has a small brown freckle on her chin, and mine is freckle free. My teeth gap in the front; hers hug each other close. Her skin is a shade darker than mine. My forehead is a little wider. Even so, there's something eerily familiar about this girl. Despite the fact she's carefully avoiding eye contact, it feels like an invisible wire connects us.

"Hey," the boy hisses again, "did you know it's bad luck to see your doppelgänger?"

My stomach drops like I just ate rocks. I'm not usually superstitious, but I ask, "What kind of bad luck?" I've already had enough bad luck.

The boy checks to see if Mrs. Ellingham is watching and then scoots his chair closer to me and Mercedes. "Some people *die* after seeing their doppelgänger."

My hands feel tingly and my heart thumps.

"Do you feel okay?" he asks me. "What did it feel like when you first saw Mercedes? Your doppelgänger?"

"Um," I say. "Weird, I guess." I don't say that it doesn't really feel like a bad-weird. Just weird.

Mercedes leans forward and hisses, "Shut up."

I'm not sure if she's talking to him or me.

"It's only a coincidence," she adds. I can tell by the squint in her brown eyes that she has decided it's bad-weird. "It didn't mean anything."

"Boys and girls!" Mrs. Ellingham claps her hands. The three of us jump. The boy scurries to his own place as the teacher says, "Look at the person sitting across from you."

We all look. Except Mercedes. Her eyes avoid mine.

"Say hello to your project partner!" Mrs. Ellingham says cheerfully.

Now Mercedes looks up. And she glares at me. Her cheeks turn bright pink. I feel my own burn. How have I managed to make enemies with a girl I've only just met and then end up partnered with her on our first big project? All on my first day in a new school? It must be my doppelgänger bad luck.

"Write both your names on the assignment and exchange phone numbers. You'll need to do some of this project outside of class. My room will always be open after school, too."

A few voices cheer, a few groan. Mercedes is one of the people groaning. Then she sighs a loud sigh that says how much she doesn't want to be my partner.

"What was your name again?" she asks, pencil poised above her paper.

"Mattie." Does she feel it? Does she feel the bad luck? "Mattie Gómez," I tell her. For one millisecond after I say my last name for the second time that day, her eyes flick to me and then back to the paper.

"How do you spell Mattie?" She emphasizes the *T*'s, sharp and jagged. Her eyes bore into me, as if I came to Poppy View Middle School just to make her life miserable. I never asked to be here. If I were still at my old school, I could be doing group projects with people who actually like me. Maybe even with my best friend, Mai. I try to picture life back home in Saint Paul, Minnesota. Soon the leaves will turn red, lopsided pumpkins drawn by first graders will be taped to the school windows, and the air will smell like the first frost.

Mercedes taps her pencil on the paper, waiting.

"Two *T*'s," I tell her. "M-A-T-T-I-E."

"It's a . . . ," she begins. She pauses as if searching for the right word. "It's a *cute* name."

"Thank—"

"My friend had a dog named Mattie," she adds.

A dog?

I smile the way I do when my mom tells me to clean my room, but I know I probably won't. "Well, it's short for Matilde." And then I spell very, very slowly, "M-A-T-I-L-D-E."

Mercedes shoots me a look that could freeze a lake in Minnesota. I shrug.

"I'm named after the wife of this famous dead poet Pablo Neruda," I inform her. "You've probably never heard of him. It was my father's idea." I'm not sure why I say that. I *never* talk about my father to anyone.

Mercedes traces the *M* in her own name over and over until it's dark and black. "I'm named after a wife, too. The wife of a famous writer."

We don't make eye contact, but the wire between us seems to buzz.

CHAPTER 2

Mercedes

The moment she walks into Mrs. Ellingham's room, I get a sinking feeling deep in my bones.

"Whoa," Gaby whispers, her breath hot in my ear. "That new girl looks just like you."

My chest burns. Gaby and I watch Mrs. Ellingham hand the girl a textbook and point her toward the only empty seat in our classroom. Across from me.

"Not really," I say, even though anyone can see that the girl and I have hair the same brown color that looks black in some light and reddish in others. We also happen to have it cut in the same style just past our shoulders. Hers is in a ponytail but I can tell it's the same curly frizz as mine. "I mean, obviously, she's never heard of a flat iron. Or been to a mall."

"Other than the hair and the, uh, weird clothes." The girl is wearing crisp, dark jeans—totally out of style—and a T-shirt that says *Lake Superior*. "There's something," Gaby insists. "I don't know—something familiar that makes her look just like you."

I shake my head, but it's obvious. There's the slight upward curve of our eyes. There's her chin—a little pointy like mine. We both have button noses, although mine is definitely cuter.

"Ha," I say with a short laugh. "I don't think so." I try my best to sound offended, like I don't know what she means. I don't want her to guess my secret.

Just then the bell rings and she returns to her spot. Gaby is my best friend, but I'm glad she's at the front of the room and I'm in the back. Mrs. Ellingham shoos people into their seats. Then she makes the new girl introduce herself. *Mattie.*

She's got to be who I think she is. Although I usually love being right, this time I wouldn't mind being wrong. What is she doing here? At Poppy View Middle School? In seventh grade? With me?

All around the classroom, kids whisper and stare at me and the girl, pointing out the obvious: that we look alike. As the girl speaks, her face turns as red as the notebook on her desk. I almost feel sorry for her. There's a sad quiver in her voice as she tells the class her name.

"Gómez," the girl says.

Gómez. I'm certain now. Just my luck.

And my luck gets worse when Mrs. Ellingham assigns partners for our next project. Me and the new girl. As I write Mattie's name on my worksheet, she tells me her father named her after some poet's wife. A zing goes through me when she says the word "father."

I know I should keep my mouth shut, but I can't help blurting out, "I'm named after a wife, too." I don't recite my whole story about not knowing my dad. Instead, I repeat, "The wife of a famous writer." I don't mention that the writer is this Colombian dude, Gabriel García Márquez, or that his wife's name was Mercedes Barcha. "I'm *not* named after a car," I add, even though she didn't ask if I was.

"Mercedes is a cool name," Mattie says.

A cool name. I almost smile. But then I look at her sloppy shirt and frizzy ponytail and think about her saying the word "father." How uncomfortable it made me feel. I don't need this girl being friendly or telling me what's cool.

She rips a piece of paper out of her notebook. "I guess we need to exchange numbers," she says, writing her name and phone number on the top half. She tears off the bottom and hands me the scrap of paper. "So we can work on our project." Her voice is low. It sounds like mine when I'm tired or trying to get Mom to buy me something expensive. In other words, it's annoying.

"Fine." I write my number on the ripped paper and hand it to her.

At lunch, Gaby and Rebecca won't leave me alone.

"I still can't believe that new girl," Gaby says. The three of us look over at Mattie, who is sitting at the lunch table with the dorkiest kids in seventh grade. I never thought I would meet her, but if I did, I always thought she would probably be a lot like me—you know, pretty cool. I never would've guessed she'd actually *look* like me . . . but *be* nothing like me.

Gaby explains to Rebecca, "She's this un-cool version of our girl. Like, if Mercedes didn't dress like Mercedes." Gaby is obsessed with clothes. She used to always ask to borrow mine, but over the summer her chest grew and my clothes don't fit her anymore. Gaby has always been the flaky one, Rebecca is the serious one, and I'm the perfect one—the one with the wealthy mom, cool shoes, cute little brother, and fun ideas.

"That's so weird! How is it even possible?" asks Rebecca, staring at Mattie Gómez from across the lunchroom. "For someone to look just like you?"

"It's called a doppelgänger." After social studies, I looked up the word on my phone. *A ghostly and often negative double of a living person.* Standing at my locker, getting jostled by the sixth graders heading to phys ed, I read the definition over and over. *Negative?* The zing I felt earlier zinged again, right into my stomach.

"A what?"

"A doppelgänger," I repeat. They both give me a funny look. Weird as it sounds, saying I have a doppelgänger seems like a better alternative than telling them the whole story.

"Doppel-what?" Rebecca says.

"She's in a gang?" asks Gaby.

Ugh. The three of us have been friends since first grade, but sometimes they can be so annoying. I explain, "A doppelgänger is someone who looks like your twin but isn't." I don't mention the bad luck part. "Like, you know how Cristina looks like Gal Gadot?"

They giggle. Ever since Mom hired a nanny to take care of my little brother, we've been arguing with her about this. Cristina insists she doesn't look anything like the movie star, but we keep telling her she does.

"Gaby, your doppelgänger is that girl in that one show," Rebecca says.

Gaby laughs harder. "You never know the names of any celebrities, do you, Becca?"

"Your doppelgänger is Zendaya!"

Phew. I'm glad they've stopped asking questions about me. About Mattie.

Gaby and Rebecca collapse in giggles. A juice box gets tipped over and we shriek as we escape the sticky mess. All the seventh graders turn and stare at us, which means it's time to put on a show, remind everyone how popular we are. I start humming our favorite song, and right away Gaby and Rebecca join in. We've been rehearsing a bunch of choreography during sleepovers this summer and we're ready. We stand up and use our bags of chips as microphones. We know all the lyrics and sing in unison. Gaby and Rebecca swing their hips to the right, to the left. I'm in the middle so I do the foot moves, in and out. "Na-na-na-na-na!" we sing. Kids around us look up from their sandwiches and laugh. The three of us coordinate our disco moves and the lunchroom audience stomps the beat. *"I'm in the stars tonight!"* I wail into my Doritos microphone. I love the feeling of being in the spotlight.

I'm about to take a big, exaggerated bow when Mrs. Leeds comes marching toward us. Uh-oh. Our principal does not like it when we're loud at lunch.

"Ladies," Mrs. Leeds says in a warning voice.

"Sorry," we say. I like being the center of attention, but I also like being a good student.

As I'm sitting down again, I spot Mattie Gómez at the dork table and our eyes catch for a split second. Something seems to connect us, like an invisible spiderweb.

CHAPTER 3

Mattie

Mattie!" I hear someone shout as I follow the other seventh graders to lunch. It's the boy with the spiky hair. The one who said it's bad luck to see your doppelgänger. "I'm in your social studies class. I'm November."

"That's your name? November?"

"Exactly. Like the month." He doesn't seem embarrassed about his name at all. "You can sit with us if you want," he continues as we enter the lunchroom. He points at a table near the back where two kids are unpacking their lunch bags. A boy with black hair that hangs over one eye and a tiny girl in pigtails. "That's Ted. That's Sunny."

I survey the landscape, looking for the place where a new kid would fit. At one end of the room, four tables are crowded with boys who pop up and down like prairie dogs. At the other end are a couple tables filled with girls—one of which includes my doppelgänger. Near November's friends are several more tables half-filled with kids. I feel an ache in my chest as I picture Mai eating lunch with our other friend Sonja instead of me. A wave of homesickness washes over me. I plop my lunch bag next to November and his two companions. Better than sitting alone.

"Has anyone told you that you look just like Mercedes Miller?" the boy with black hair says.

"I know, right, Ted?" November says. "They're both in my social studies class—you can hardly tell them apart."

The girl in pigtails named Sunny says something I can't understand. "What?"

"You look like twins," she says. Her voice is squeaky like she doesn't use it much. "Are you related?"

Sunny is just one more kid who has asked if I'm related to Mercedes Miller today. Social studies, then English, then science. Ms. Garcia, the science teacher, kept calling me, "Mer—Mattie," as if that was my new name. *Mer-Mattie.* Like I'm some kind of sea creature.

"Never seen her before in my life," I tell my lunchmates, returning to my sandwich. Just as I take a bite, November asks, "Where are you from, Mattie?"

People are always asking me where I'm from, especially when they see me with my mom. She has light-brown hair and blue eyes; I have dark hair and brown eyes. She's tall and angular; I'm still growing and have a bit of what Mai's grandma calls "baby fat." My mom—and her family for five generations—is from Minnesota. My father is from Colombia. The one in South America. I've never been there. Or met him.

"I was born in Santa Cruz," November volunteers while I chew, "and Ted is from Los Angeles. Sunny is from Oklahoma. How about you?"

Oh. "Minnesota."

Sunny mumbles something.

"What?" I ask.

Sunny squeaks, "I was new last year."

"And I was new in fifth grade," Ted tells me.

"I'm the welcoming committee," November says. "We take in new kids." He looks from Ted to Sunny. "If you want."

Do I want a welcoming committee? Do I need one? I think about the two weeks with my new stepfamily before my mom and Bob's wedding. That was supposed to be our welcoming vacation. The five of us stayed in a rented cabin in the woods in northern Minnesota. There was a lake and a boat with a motor that spat black smoke, and there were loons calling in the evenings. Five-year-old Lucas kept asking if we were in Canada. Even though it was a nice place with a good view and a firepit for s'mores, the vacation didn't feel very welcoming. My two soon-to-be stepbrothers didn't have much to say to me. Lucas discovered dock fishing and smelled like dead fish most of the time. And it wasn't until my mom found an old chess set in a cupboard that Kenny acknowledged my existence. That's when I found out he belongs to a chess club, just like Mai and I did in fifth grade. He still wasn't exactly welcoming, but at least he couldn't completely ignore me while we were playing chess—especially when I checkmated him.

I glance at the other lunch tables, at kids I don't know who don't care who I am, at the girl who looks like me but is carefully not paying attention to me. I guess I could use a welcoming committee. "Oh, okay," I say to November. "Thanks."

"Where in Minnesota are you from?" Ted asks.

"Saint Paul."

"That's the capital city."

"Ted knows all the capitals," November explains.

"Montana: Helena; North Dakota: Bismarck; Idaho: Boise; Colorado: Denver," Ted says in one breath. I'm impressed.

November grins. "He's a walking Wikipedia."

Ted taps his head. "Steel trap."

"Isn't it super cold in Minnesota?" Sunny squeaks.

"Brrr." November makes a shivering noise. "Snow, right?"

"Not all the time," I say. "It can be really nice—"

We're interrupted by a commotion from across the lunchroom. My doppelgänger and her friends stand and start singing a song I probably should know but don't. They're doing some dance that involves a lot of hip shaking and stomping. They belt out the song at the top of their lungs. They look ridiculous—but also kind of cool. Like *High School Musical* is happening live at Poppy View Middle School.

"Mercedes Miller and her gang love attention," November says. "Any kind. Watch."

The moment he says this, a woman in a blue suit appears in the lunchroom. She strides to their table. "Ladies," she says, tapping each girl on her shoulder, making them each sit. My doppelgänger is the last one. "Lunch period is for eating, not dancing."

"That's Mrs. Leeds, the principal," November explains to me.

Mrs. Leeds looks around the room. "This is middle school, not elementary school. We expect better behavior. Next time you decide to put on a show, you'll be sorting recycling."

Mrs. Leeds strolls across the lunchroom. If I were them, I would be so embarrassed. But as soon as she's gone, the girls stand up one more time. They bow in unison, like they choreographed the whole thing. Kids around us applaud.

I keep my eye on Mercedes Miller. She flips her hair and

shakes her wrist so that her bracelets jangle. Her sneakers match her mint-green nails. For one second, she glances at me. The bite of sandwich in my mouth suddenly tastes like cardboard. There's something about Mercedes Miller that makes me want to hate her. And something else about her that makes me want to get to know her better.

The next morning, when I grab my phone from the living room where my mom makes me charge it overnight, there's a text waiting for me.

Good luck on your 2nd day!

I smile so big, just like I do every time I hear from Mai. She's been my best friend since kindergarten. I needed this message with the yellow flower, green heart, unicorn, and shooting star. Mai loves emojis. At least this one thing is the same from my old life.

And I really need something normal this morning. I'm dreading my second day. All night I tossed and turned. My pillow kept falling on the floor and my blanket kept slipping sideways. When I did finally fall asleep, I dreamed I was trying to open my locker in an underwater school. I woke up feeling soggy.

When I go to the kitchen for breakfast, no one in my new family notices me at first, not even my mom. She's sipping coffee and staring out the window at the gray clouds.

"He's widowed," she told me before I met Bob for the first time. "You know what that means?"

I nodded. *Did* I know what that meant? "Um, but you can explain it," I said.

"It means his wife died. She died when his youngest was three years old. He has two kids." At the time, I hadn't even known if he had girls or boys. I had hoped there were girls, of course. What only child hasn't wished for a sister?

Instead, I got stepbrothers. Two of them.

Ten-year-old Kenny is dripping Cheerios and milk all over the Batman comic book he's reading. My stepdad, Bob, is buttering his youngest son's bread.

"Toast," Bob says to Lucas.

"Most!" rhymes Lucas. He laughs like it's the most hilarious thing in the world.

"Jam?"

"Ham!" shouts Lucas. I'm already learning that Lucas never speaks, only shouts.

More laughing.

"Thumb," says Bob, licking jelly off his fingers.

Dumb, I think to myself. I don't dare say it aloud. I glance at my mom.

"There you are," she says, noticing her only daughter at last. "Ready for day two?"

"I am!" shouts Lucas, who has decided he loves kindergarten.

"I'm just glad we got two extra weeks of vacation," says Kenny.

I have to agree with him. Due to my mom's confusion and Bob's absentmindedness, all three of us missed the first two weeks of school.

"But school always starts *after* Labor Day!" my mom said when we were still at the rented cabin and Kenny had said how excited he was to miss school for the wedding.

"Not in California," Kenny said. "The first day for the elementary school was yesterday. Probably the same for her." Kenny shrugged his shoulder in my direction. Even though we had been playing chess for ten days by then, he still avoided looking directly at me.

"Did you know about this?" My mom looked at Bob.

"I'm going to miss kindergarten?" Lucas cried.

"Oh, darn," Kenny said in a sarcastic tone. "Guess I'll have to miss the first two weeks of fifth grade."

"Doh!" said Bob. "I'm sorry, guys. I guess I'm just so excited to marry Valerie, I forgot all about school. Should we move the wedding?"

My mom laughed. "We can't change the wedding, Bob. It's in less than a week!"

But I didn't like the idea of starting school late. I knew I was going to stick out. But, of course, I hadn't realized how much.

And now, here I am, starting my second day of seventh grade during what was the other students' second week. On top of that, a gray cloud swirls depressingly outside the kitchen window. "Why is it so . . . gross outside?" I ask.

"It's just morning fog," Bob says.

"Bog!" shouts Lucas.

"Nice job, kiddo." Bob laughs. To me, he adds, "It should clear later today. Or sometimes morning fog lasts a few days."

"Maze!"

I ignore Lucas. "Then why is it called morning fog?"

"It makes people feel better," he says with a smile.

"Letter!"

I do not feel better.

And I don't feel any better when I arrive at Poppy View for day two. Just like yesterday, kids whisper and point as I pass them in the corridors. *Mer-mattie*, I hear, still feeling like I'm under water.

While I'm taking out my textbooks at my locker and putting my phone away, I hear a piercing shriek. The lockers are lined up along an outdoor corridor that connects the classrooms, which are really just little buildings of their own. Back home in Minnesota, schools are enclosed, often red brick, the gray metal lockers in stuffy hallways with flickering fluorescent lighting. Here the breeze from the ocean smells like salt and cold water, and the lockers are painted the school colors—red and yellow. There's the shriek again. Across the corridor, Mercedes Miller giggles with her gang of girls. One thing that isn't different from Minnesota is that there are always popular kids. And Mercedes Miller and her friends are clearly popular. They all have matching bracelets and headbands today. Mercedes's nails are painted tangerine orange. The girls' echoey laughter makes me feel even more alone. I miss Mai so much.

By the time I get to gym class in the afternoon, I'm antsy. There was a pop quiz in math, a boring movie in social studies, and a slow read-aloud in English. The whispers and questions continued in between all of the seventh-grade schoolwork. *Are you related? Are you her cousin? Are you twins?* I'm hoping we're going to do something easy, like jump rope. I follow the other students to the big field beyond the basketball hoops. At my old school, this class would be held in a big gym with wooden floorboards. I spot November and Sunny from lunch and stand awkwardly next to them while the teacher gets organized.

"Hi," I say to Sunny. She gives me a smile as small as she is.

"You guys ready?" November asks. The whole welcoming committee is in my phys ed class.

"Ready for what?" I ask, squinting in the bright sun. Bob was right—no sign of fog this afternoon.

Sunny mumbles something.

"What?"

"Mile run," she squeaks.

The mile run? I'm not *that* antsy.

"Are you as fast as Mercedes Miller? She's the fastest girl in our class," November informs me.

"I'm not fast at all," I say. In fact, I was the slowest kid in the whole sixth grade last year. I broke a record for the slowest time ever.

"Wait till you see Sunny. She's second fastest."

Sunny looks embarrassed. "I like running."

I hate running. I don't like the way my lungs burn or my chest constricts—it's too much like having a panic attack. Just thinking about running makes my jaw clench, my toes curl. My stomach churns. I close my eyes. *Relax*, I tell myself.

"I thought maybe you were fast, too, Mattie," November says. I open my eyes. "Since you look so much like Mercedes."

I don't want to run the mile. But I do wish I could run away.

CHAPTER 4

Mercedes

D on't get lost," Mr. Martin says as he tells us the route for the mile run. As if it were even possible to get off course when we're just running around the school. "Follow the orange cones around the field, past the parking lot, in front of the office, and back around on the sidewalk to the basketball courts."

I stretch out my calves, lunging on first one leg, then the other. The more warmed up you are, the better your chances. "Aren't you going to stretch?" I ask Gaby.

"Nah," she says, tugging at her shorts. "I run after Lori and Luke enough." Gaby babysits for her hyperactive brother and sister whenever her mom has to drive her other brothers to work at the mall. "Do you think that girl who looks just like you is as fast as you?"

"Who?" I ask, even though I know exactly who she's talking about. I saw her leaving gym class just as we arrived. She was red-faced and sweaty. There's no way she's as good a runner as I am.

"You know, that weird new girl?" Gaby laughs. I just shrug. The less I talk about her, the better.

"Remember," Mr. Martin announces to the class, "you're just trying to improve from your last time."

"That won't be hard for me," says Gaby, giggling. She never takes anything seriously. Schoolwork, sports, nothing. She just goes with the flow—which, in the case of the mile run, isn't very fast. Sometimes that's what I love about her (especially when she's going along with whatever I say), but sometimes it drives me crazy. "I don't even remember my last score," she says.

I know exactly how fast I need to go if I want to beat my last time of six minutes, fifty-two seconds. During the mile run last year, I beat the fastest boy, Joaquin, because his shoe came untied and he tripped. My plan is to beat him again.

"This isn't a competition," Mr. Martin says. He readjusts his hat and then brings his whistle to his lips.

I crouch down and tighten my shoelaces. Even if it's not a competition, when you're known as the fastest runner, you have to beat your time—and everyone else's.

"Runners, take your marks!"

My body tenses, ready to go. The rush of blood pounds in my ears. From somewhere, like in a dream, I hear the teacher shout, "GO!"

I catapult forward. I pump my arms, move my legs. I forget about Gaby and Joaquin. My mind loosens, concentrates only on the path in front of me. I keep Mr. Martin's orange cones to my right as I race along the outside of the field, run toward the parking lot. I love the feeling of the turn as my body leans and balances.

"Mercedes!" I hear Gaby shout, but I ignore her.

"Think you're fast just 'cause you're named after a car?" someone just inches away from me says. From the corner of my eye, I can see that it's Joaquin, trying to beat me this time. He thinks he's so funny. But I won't let anyone distract me.

Not even Mattie Gómez. Not only do our faces look alike, we're also about the same height with the same long legs. I wonder if she *is* as fast as me, if she also likes the feeling of letting go as you run like a wild horse.

To my left, someone is passing me. It's Dante now. My pace has slowed. This is all Mattie's fault! Why did she have to appear in my city? At my school? In my grade? At least we don't have phys ed together.

I want to scream, but instead I take that jolt of energy and transfer it to my running. My legs thrum, propelling me forward. I push thoughts of Mattie away. I gain on Joaquin and Dante. Like I always do, I concentrate on moving forward, on achieving my goal. And I keep running.

"Are you okay?" Cristina asks as she bites into her tofu. We're at my nanny's favorite Vietnamese restaurant. We eat here every Tuesday while we wait to pick up my little brother from his dad's.

I never go to *my* dad's house. I mean, maybe if I had ever met him, I would. But I'm not one of those kids with the split custody thing like Tristan—every Tuesday night and every other weekend.

I dip my eggroll in sesame sauce. Should I tell Cristina about Mattie? If I tell her about Matilde Gómez, though, she might tell Mom.

"I'm fine." Instead, I tell her how I beat my best time in the mile run. "Six minutes, thirty-seven seconds." I don't tell her that even though I should be having the best day ever because I beat Joaquin again, I can't get Mattie Gómez out of my mind. She's ruining my day. I'm pretty sure she might be ruining my life, too.

After dinner, Cristina drives us back to pick up Tristan at his dad's apartment. She waits in the driveway while I knock on the door to get my brother.

"Sorry, Mercedes," Tristan's dad says when he opens it. "He's not ready yet. Come on in."

This is what happens every week. Cristina waits in the car and I wait for Tristan. He's never ready. This, as Mom always says, is all his dad's fault. His dad is a nice guy but totally unorganized. His apartment is a disaster. Even if you don't count Tristan's stuff, which is scattered around the living room like a toy store exploded. A coloring book, one sock, two racecars, a packet of markers with the green and blue missing (his two favorite colors). While I wait, I study the pictures above the sofa, just like I do every time I'm here. The wall is covered in mismatched frames, each of them with photos of Tristan. There's Tristan's newborn baby picture; there's him with his first tooth. There's Tristan on a donkey at a petting zoo. There's Tristan and his dad on a sailboat, and one of them squeezed together on a bus seat. I pretend not to be looking for the small frame at the far end of the wall. In it, a six-year-old Mercedes smiles with a baby Tristan. The hand on my shoulder in the picture belongs to his dad. I remember Mom taking this picture and thinking that Tristan's dad was *my* dad.

I look around at the messy apartment. When Tristan's dad lived with us, our house had family photos on the walls, too.

And it was just as cluttered. Maybe it was his messiness that made Mom mad. "It's just not working," Mom said three years ago and then he moved out.

"Finally ready," Tristan's dad says, handing me Tristan's backpack at last.

"Bye," I say awkwardly. I never use his name. He's always been "Tristan's dad." As if he had nothing to do with me. He's Tristan's dad, not mine. The sooner I forget about him—like Mom has—the better.

My brother waves and calls out, "Bye, Daddy!"

I help him buckle his booster seat, even though he can totally do it himself now. As I climb in the passenger seat, Tristan's dad waves to him from the door.

After he moved out, Mom redecorated—not that she's ever around to see it. "It feels so much more spacious in here, doesn't it?" she said after decluttering and rearranging the living room. Duh, I thought. What really made it feel more spacious was the fact that there was one less person in our family. She covered the walls in oil paintings and artisan baskets and filled display cases with Chinese pottery and archaeological artifacts. And all our family photos disappeared.

Sometimes I'm not sure she'd even notice if *I* disappeared.

CHAPTER 5

Mattie

Your school pictures seem to have disappeared," my mom says when I get home from school. She's on our turquoise sofa in the living room, surrounded by boxes. "I'm making an album for each of you." She holds up a stack of photo albums. "And a wedding album!"

I have my mom to myself for twenty minutes before Lucas and Kenny get off the bus. I sit on the floor and leaf through the boxes. There's a pile of pictures from the wedding—just snapshots; they didn't hire a photographer. Photos of Lucas and Kenny are mixed together in different cardboard boxes. "How can you tell them apart?" I ask, holding up two baby pictures of blond-haired boys.

My mom laughs. "I'll have Bob help with those. I'm starting with yours. Look." She hands me a half-filled book. I've seen the pictures before, but they were always kept in an old shoebox. "You were such a cute baby."

I study one of my baby pictures. My cheeks are round and fat. My hair is black and flops over my forehead. I slip the photo out of the book and turn it over. *Matilde, 10 months.* I sneak it into my pocket; it's *my* picture, after all.

"Oh, here they are!" My mom opens a creased envelope

and dumps the pictures on the couch cushion. First grade: missing front teeth; second grade: pigtails; third grade: Mickey Mouse T-shirt. She laughs and holds up my fourth-grade picture. I'm scowling and my face is pale, my nose red. "You were so sick that day. I should never have let you go to school."

"I remember," I say. "I didn't want to miss picture day."

"You never like to change plans, do you, Mattie-mouse?"

I nod as she fits the school pictures into the pages of my book. Everywhere I look are changes. The living room is a mix of old and new, past and present. It has our sofa—but also Bob's zigzag rug and ugly painting of a moose. Lucas's red ball is on our striped chair and Kenny's chess set is on Bob's coffee table. It's like I'm stuck in this weird place that is kind of like home but isn't at all familiar.

When my mom first started dating Bob, I really didn't think it would last. After all, our life was in Minnesota and his was in California. Separate. But then Bob and his kids came for Thanksgiving last year and then we went to Santa Cruz for winter break. It started to feel real, even though we all still felt like strangers. When Bob gave her a sparkly diamond ring, I thought maybe the Jaspers would move to Minnesota. All that changed when my mom got laid off from the marketing job she hated, and the lease ended on our house, and she decided she wanted a change.

"We can have a fresh start in California, Mattie-mouse."

I nodded, but I didn't want a fresh start. What twelve-year-old needs a fresh start?

"And no more winters!" she tried, but I love snow.

"Bob has orange trees in the backyard!" she said, as if this were a selling point.

But seeing the way my mom looks at this goofy, tall, bearded man and the way he looks at her makes me wonder. Oranges and no snowy winters will never make up for leaving my friends, my life, my home, but seeing my mom happy might.

"This is going on the last page." My mom holds out a photo of the two of us. I'm in two tight braids and the yellow sundress she picked out for me, and she's in her white linen wedding dress. I remember going to the tailor with her to get it shortened. Before the wedding and the move to California, it felt like all we did was errands. We took lots of trips to the donation center, where we got rid of a dresser, two armchairs, our old red dishes, and our blackened pots and pans.

"Bob has all this stuff," my mom told me. "I don't know about you, but I'm ready for new dishes." I wasn't so sure. I still remember eating my mom's homemade birthday cake off the chipped red plates. The big bowls were the ones we filled with popcorn for movie nights. My mom always used the mug with the broken handle for chicken soup when I was sick. When we were packing up that old stuff, I couldn't imagine life without the dishes. I couldn't imagine a life where I'd have to share my mom. Actually, I hadn't been able to imagine life in California at all. All I could think about was what I was losing.

"It was such a pretty wedding, wasn't it, Mattie-mouse?" my mom asks, cradling the photo in her palm. I nod. The wedding wasn't like a wedding in a movie—it wasn't in a big church, just in the backyard of our house in Saint Paul. Someone took this photo of us right after we ate cake. I can tell because I have a smear of frosting on my cheek. But my mom looks perfect. Beautiful. And happy. I'm certain I've never seen her this happy. She's squeezing me so hard. Just looking at the photo, I can feel her tight grip on my shoulders.

She tucks the photo into the plastic sleeve of the last page of my book, like it's the happily-ever-after part. With mine finished, the other albums are ready to be filled with strangers' stories. I think about my new school, the new people. Whether I like it or not, this might be the beginning of a story, not the ending.

"Yours is done," my mom says. She pushes my photo album aside to make room for the next one just as Lucas and Kenny barge through the front door.

Amazingly, I survive day three at Poppy View. Social studies with Mercedes Miller staring at me from across the desk. Lunch with my welcoming committee. Math, where I learn how far behind I am. Now I just need to make it through my afterschool mythology study session with Mercedes Miller.

I check the clock in Mrs. Ellingham's room. Mercedes was supposed to meet me here at three ten. It's three fifteen now. Mrs. Ellingham left to make copies, so I pace the empty room alone. On the cinderblock walls I spot a sign on the bulletin board that says ASK WHAT YOU CAN DO FOR YOUR COUNTRY in big red and blue letters, a colorful map of the world, and a list of classroom rules, which includes NO GUM, NO HATS, AND ALWAYS BRING A SMILE. I'm definitely not smiling now.

"Good, you're here." Mercedes Miller slams the classroom door shut behind her in a huff, like I'm the one who's late. She's wearing running shorts, electric-blue sneakers, and a sweatshirt with a brand name across the front—not a cute cat picture like mine. Her fingernails are pale blue. Watching her smooth hair swing around her shoulders, I yank my frizzy ponytail tighter. I wish I could get my hair to do that.

"Did you read through the myths?" she asks, dropping her navy-and-pink backpack on the floor. It's covered in buttons from state parks and camps. It's dirty but in a cool, I'm-super-busy-and-active kind of way. "Which one do you think we should do?"

I open the mythology packet. I studied Greek myths last year at my old school, so I'm hoping we can choose one I didn't learn about. But I can already tell that Mercedes is going to take over. There's something about Mercedes that makes her hard to contradict.

"We should do the Selene story. The one about the moon," Mercedes says.

I was right. She's taking over.

"No one else will do that one. Besides, it'll be easy to do a cool report. We can do a diorama with lights. I know just what to do." She taps her blue fingernails on the desk.

I open my packet to the story. "Don't you think it's kind of . . . " I'm not sure how to say that I don't want to do that one. "Boring?"

"Boring?" Mercedes looks at me like I just suggested walking around naked.

"Yeah," I say. "Selene has got to be the most boring myth of all." I point to the story. "Listen to this: '*Selene, one of the Titans, was the goddess of the moon. Each night she drove her silver chariot pulled by two white horses across the sky. Her brother, Helios, was the god of the sun, and he drove a golden chariot carried by four horses across the sky each day.'"* I look up at Mercedes. "See? She's only interesting because of who her brother was! And, look, the moon only gets two horses while the sun gets four. Totally unfair."

"Selene is the *moon* goddess. And that's cool."

"But she doesn't *do* anything."

"But she's a cool woman. In a Greek myth." Mercedes fans the pages of the packet. "There are hardly any myths about women. And we should be, you know, all about hashtag-women's-rights and hashtag-girl-power."

"But—," I begin. I can tell there's probably no point in even trying to argue with Mercedes, but I can't help it. I repeat, "Selene doesn't *do* anything."

"Yes, she does. She drives a chariot around the moon. She *is* the moon. Don't you know that the moon controls the tides?"

I think of the ocean that hugs the city of Santa Cruz, and it makes me miss the Mississippi River in Minnesota.

"Selene's super powerful."

"Is she?" I ask. "I mean, the moon might be powerful, but what about her? She doesn't *do* anything as the moon. No purpose. Her brother Helios is way more powerful. What about Hera?" I try. "She's a girl."

"Ugh!" Mercedes groans. "Hera's always trying to get revenge."

Mercedes and I stare at each other.

"We're doing Selene." Her voice is cold and hard.

There are those eyes again.

"Besides," she adds breezily, "I don't think it matters. We're getting graded on our projects and my idea for a night sky diorama will be an A-plus project for sure."

I blink. Her brown eyes are so familiar, like looking in a mirror. "Fine," I say at last. There really is something about Mercedes that makes you agree with her. Even if you don't want to.

"That's settled," she says, and pulls a beat-up three-ring binder from her backpack. I open my folder, which is still shiny and new in a very uncool way.

"We'll do this section first," Mercedes commands. Out the window of Mrs. Ellingham's classroom, fog creeps in. My mom loves the fog—she loves everything about California. Personally, I don't like the way the fog hides everything familiar, like it's keeping secrets from you.

"Matilde," Mercedes barks. No one ever calls me that. I regret spelling out my full name for her. "Concentrate." She points to the clock above the whiteboard. "My ride is coming in thirty minutes."

My mom is picking me up soon, too, so I get to work.

When Mrs. Ellingham returns with a stack of photocopies under her arm, Mercedes and I are silent, bent over our packets. "Well!" Mrs. Ellingham says. "Look at you two."

I jerk in surprise and so does Mercedes. My doppelgänger is sitting in the exact same position as I am. Left leg tucked, right elbow on the table. We both stop jiggling our right feet at the same time.

"You two could be sisters," Mrs. Ellingham says brightly.

I'm about to say something to the teacher about

doppelgängers. But then I see Mercedes's face flush red. Not just her cheeks but her neck, too. As red as our old dishes. She stands up so quickly, she knocks her pencils, binder, and Greek myths packet to the floor.

"Sorry to startle you," Mrs. Ellingham says with a short laugh. "I'll let you get back to work." She settles at her desk at the back of the room, hidden behind a stack of books, a pile of papers, and a large file organizer.

I crouch next to Mercedes, helping her gather everything that scattered across the floor. When I pick up her binder, I pause to study it. Somehow, she's taken a plain pink binder and made it look cool. It's disorganized but artsy. Photos and drawings are tucked underneath the clear plastic cover. There are printed-out selfies of her and other girls I don't recognize, photos of a fluffy gray cat. She outlined some of the pictures with Sharpie over the plastic, creating little frames. There is just the right amount of gold puffy-paint polka dots and stars. And then something else catches my eye.

Mercedes reaches for the binder. Her fingers grip it, turning white at the knuckles. But even as she tugs on it, I don't let it go. I just keep staring at it. And not only because it's so pretty. I stare because there, tucked under the plastic and nearly hidden by the arc of a hand-drawn rainbow, is a familiar face.

My mouth goes dry. "Who's that?" I ask, pointing a trembling finger at the photo. At the man's face.

"No one you would know." She yanks the binder out of my hands, leaving a bright-pink scrape across my palm.

Even though the snapshot is behind scuffed plastic and elaborately framed in a geometric design, I recognize it. I recognize it the same way I recognized Mercedes's nose, the same way I recognized Mercedes's hair. I recognize the face of Francisco Gómez, smiling at me in the exact same way he smiles from the picture I have of him on my dresser at home.

My father.

CHAPTER 6

Mercedes

S ometimes just one choice can make all the difference. If I could go back in time, change a choice I'd made, I wouldn't have put that photo of Frank Gómez in my binder. I'm not even sure why I did it.

I found the picture when I was looking for a glue stick for Tristan. We were making a WELCOME HOME banner for Mom. It was Cristina's idea to surprise her. That was when Mom first started traveling so much. I didn't see the point in welcoming her home; she was just going to leave again. Tristan was five years old and super excited about gluing glitter on the banner. I was digging around the drawer in the kitchen among the takeout menus and old rubber bands when I found the photo. Mom had showed it to me a couple times when I was little, whenever I asked about who my father was. The story she told me every time was that he lived in Colombia, that he was too busy and important for children. I hadn't seen the photo since we first moved to the big Santa Cruz house. On the back of the picture, it said *Frank Gomez* in Mom's neat printing. I flipped it over again and looked at the face, and then I sneaked it into the pocket of my sweatshirt. If Mom noticed it was missing, she never said anything. Not that she was ever around to notice. Even when she's not traveling for work—which is most of the time lately—she's at her fancy office in the city. I kept the photo in my desk drawer hidden under my pencil box.

At least I thought it was hidden until last Christmas, when my nosy little brother uncovered the picture while trying to find where we'd hidden his presents. "What's this?" he asked, studying the face of Frank Gómez.

"Um," I stalled. I wasn't sure what to tell him. And then I decided to tell him the truth because that's all I ever want. The truth. "That's my dad."

Tristan stared at me, mouth sagging open. "What about Daddy?"

"He's *your* dad, Tristan, not mine. We have different dads."

"Then . . ." He paused. "Are you still my sister?"

"Of course. I'll always be Tristan Miller's big sister. And you're my brother."

"How come you never go to your dad's house for the weekend like I do?"

"Oh, he lives too far away," I said.

"You can come with me," Tristan offered. "I can share Daddy with you."

I ruffled my brother's sandy hair. "That's okay; you keep your dad to yourself. I'm fine." But my heart felt like an arrow had just gone through it. What if I got to spend weekends and holidays with my own dad, I wondered. What was he like? Was he fun and disorganized like Tristan's dad or energetic and a workaholic like Mom? Sometimes I imagine that Mom has the story wrong, that he does like children, that someday he would come to California just to meet me. Sometimes I put his picture next to one of Mom and try to imagine them together. It's impossible.

Once, I searched the web for him, but there were so many people with the same name, it was impossible to tell if any of these Frank Gómezes was my father. I knew he wasn't a lawyer in New Jersey or a soccer player in Mexico. I was pretty sure he wasn't a high school student in Toronto or a retired soldier in Washington, DC.

Later, when I was decorating my seventh-grade binder, I slipped the photo under the plastic cover, partly hiding it behind a rainbow sticker. I didn't think anyone would notice the man with the messy hair, brown skin, and half-open mouth. I don't know why, but I liked knowing it was there. No one had ever asked about the photo.

Until Mattie.

"Who's that?" she asks. She's sort of greenish, like she might throw up. I do *not* need her throwing up. Gross.

I quickly yank the binder away, leaving a bright red mark across her hand. Oops. "No one you would know," I lie.

"Let me see that," she insists.

Why can't she mind her own business? If I explode, it'll be all her fault.

The color is coming back into her cheeks. Her face is now as pink as the stupid binder. "I want to see that picture."

We stare at each other. I don't want her to see Frank Gómez. I don't want her to recognize him. I don't want her to realize what connects us, me and her.

Her brown eyes flash. I know what she's going to do even before she does it, but that doesn't make me move any quicker.

Fast as a lizard darting under a bush, she snatches the binder out of my hands before I can stop her. A few math papers flutter to the floor.

"Give it back," I hiss.

She hugs it to her chest and shakes her head. Then we both freeze as Mrs. Ellingham clears her throat. She doesn't look up.

"Who is this?" Mattie asks, her voice low. Her finger taps the plastic over Frank Gómez's face. "Tell me."

"I don't have to tell you anything."

"Yes. You. Do."

When I first saw this girl, she looked so quiet and wimpy. Maybe she's more like me than I thought. Right now, there's a scary look in her eyes—even if she does have a ridiculous cute kitten on her shirt. I'm not sure what to do.

"Why?" I demand. At least I can slow her down.

"Because I know who that is," she says.

What does she know? She doesn't know who I am, so she can't know much. *He's never coming back to the US, so there's no point in thinking about him.* That's what Mom said. *You've got me.* She told me that after the first time I tried to run away. She had just returned from a trip to Germany. I was ten and so mad that she was leaving again. I told her I hated her and bolted out the front door. I remember I was wearing flip-flops, so I couldn't run very fast. When she caught up with me, I yelled, "Why can't I just go live with Frank Gómez?"

"You've got me," Mom had said. And then she bought me a pair of ultra-light running shoes.

Mattie closes her eyes. "I know that's Francisco Gómez," she says in a whisper.

My stomach lurches at the sound of his name spoken out loud. Spoken by someone other than me. Someone other than Mom. His full name. His real name. *He's much too busy. Just forget about him,* Mom had said that day I ran away. I hadn't been able to forget about him. Then I guess I asked one too many times, because a few months ago she said she was sick of answering questions. *Just stop asking about him.*

"He's . . . he's my father," Mattie says. Her voice is shaking.

This is the bomb I've been waiting for since I first saw her three days ago. It feels like that explosion goes off in my stomach. For this stranger—a stranger who looks like me, but still a stranger—to say those words. *My father.* I want to scream.

She squints. I can't tell if she's angry or about to cry. Maybe both. She doesn't look so good, like maybe she's going to faint or something.

"Give it back," I say, a little louder than I mean to. This is all her fault for seeing the picture. I wish I could hide it, change the choice I made. I wish I could undo this whole moment: Mattie seeing the picture, her realizing. I wish she never came to Poppy View.

"Are you two doing okay?" asks Mrs. Ellingham, peering over her messy desk at us. "Do you need help with anything?"

I plop into my chair. Mattie does too. "We're fine," we say. In unison.

Ugh. I hate that we keep doing that.

"Mercedes." Mattie speaks low, slow. "Why do you have a picture of my father?"

There are so many stories and excuses I could tell her. *It's a free country. I cut that picture out of a magazine. I don't know who it is. The guy in the photo is your dad's doppelgänger.* But I can't say any of that. Matilde Gómez stares at me. I have to tell the truth. Her eyes, the pupils black as the night sky. Oh, boy, here we go.

"Listen, I don't have a picture of *your* dad," I say slowly so she'll understand. "I have a picture of *my* dad. Frank Gómez."

CHAPTER 7

Mattie

The words don't make any sense. Nothing makes sense. The classroom spins like I'm in a whirling black hole. My lungs don't seem to work right. Mrs. Ellingham says something, but it's like I don't even speak English anymore.

"Are you going to faint?" Mercedes hisses. Her forehead is wrinkled in either concern or anger; I can't tell which. She glances at Mrs. Ellingham and adds in a whisper, "Ugh, please don't faint."

I've only fainted once in my life. I had to get a wart on my foot removed. My mom took me to the doctor and held my hand while the doctor held my foot. It wasn't the pain, it was the fear of the pain that made me faint. I remember feeling dizzy and then sick. Out of control. I hate feeling out of control. I hate being out of control. I am *not* going to faint.

"Francisco Gómez," I say firmly, "is my father. And that's him." I point at her binder again even though she's stuffing it into her backpack and I can't see the picture now.

"You're right. That's Frank Gómez." She sighs like this is the most obvious thing in the world. "We have the same dad."

We have the same dad? The same father? Francisco Gómez?

My Colombian father who I've never met, who I never see? *How is that even possible?* I think.

"How is that even possible?" I say out loud. The photo I have of Francisco Gómez is in a black metal frame on my dresser. It's always been in my room somewhere, for as long as I can remember. I packed it in a box in Minnesota and unpacked it again in California. I walk past it every day, and mostly I don't even notice it. Like the way you know you have an elbow, but you don't think about it much. It's just there. Until you bang it on the kitchen counter, then you remember. The photo on my dresser is just the face of someone who is my father. The father I don't know. A zing goes up my spine. My mom. My father. "Wait." A terrible, horrible thought occurs to me. "My parents had *two* kids?"

Mercedes rolls her eyes. "People can have the same dad and different moms."

Oh. Right. The zing zings away.

"I mean, my brother and I have different dads," Mercedes explains. "Tristan is seven and"—she holds up a dark-brown chunk of her flat-ironed hair—"he has blond hair, blue eyes."

She flips her hair and slings her backpack over her shoulder. "Thanks, Mrs. Ellingham!" Mercedes calls as she heads for the door.

"Wait!" I call to Mercedes, grabbing my stuff. She's leaving? Now? I need more time. The clock above the whiteboard ticks toward four o'clock. My mom will be here in a few minutes.

"Anytime, girls." Mrs. Ellingham smiles like today is a regular day, not a day when a total stranger has a picture of your father in her notebook.

"Listen, Mattie," Mercedes says when we're outside the

classroom. "We have different moms. And we have the same dad." She says it so matter-of-factly.

"But—"

She speed walks toward the front entrance, her sneakers silent on the tiles of the breezeway. The sunlight churns through the evening fog like it's watching us, making strange shadows across the buildings. I run after her. I feel so out of place. I shouldn't be here. In this school. I shouldn't be in California. I shouldn't be chasing a girl who looks like me and says we have the same father.

And then I realize something. I stop. I'm panting.

"Wait!" I call again. She doesn't stop. "Mercedes, wait!" I yell. I run past the red-and-yellow lockers and the closed classroom doors and the custodian emptying trash cans. I catch up to her and grab the strap of her bag just as we reach the driveway. A girl I recognize from math class climbs in a two-door car with a rusty hood.

"If we have the same father," I say after the rusty car pulls away, "does that mean—?" I gasp. "That means we're sisters?"

Mercedes jerks her bag out of my hand. She walks to the yellow railing along the school driveway and perches on the top bar. "*Half* sisters," she says, and pulls her phone out of her pocket.

I pause. I don't think I'm coordinated enough to sit balanced on that railing, so I collapse on the curb instead. I glance over at Mercedes. Her face is partially hidden by her hair, but her expression is a mixture of annoyance and sadness and fury and maybe—or I might be imagining it—a bit of joy.

I hear a car, but it's not my mom's new minivan. Mercedes

looks up too. A tall boy climbs in and the car drives away.

Three kids emerge from the multipurpose room, laughing and talking. A black truck stops and the boys clamber inside. One of them calls to her. Mercedes pretends not to notice.

I check my phone. Four minutes after four. My mom is late to pick me up. I try not to panic. Starting in third grade, I used to get panic attacks at least once a week. Sometimes I cried; a couple times I even threw up. When it happened in school, I almost always told the teacher I was dying. The school nurse would call my mom and she'd have to explain, "She's not sick. She's having an anxiety attack." Panic *episode*, she started to call them. Because, technically, she says, they don't attack me. My mom says that if I start feeling worried, I should count backward from ten and then make a plan. *Ten, nine, eight.* A plan. My plan is to call if she doesn't show up in six more minutes.

I guess Mercedes's ride is late, too. The two of us sit ten feet apart, but we might as well be a million miles apart.

I wonder who will pick her up. Her mom? Does she have a stepdad, like I do? She said she has a brother. I open my mouth to ask her. My phone pings. It's my mom texting me that Bob is picking me up. I'm so surprised, I call her. "Why can't you come?" I ask. Even I can hear the whining in my voice. She explains that Bob's getting Kenny from soccer practice and Poppy View Middle School is on the way home. After twelve years of being an only child, how did I end up with a stepfather who picks me up from school? And stepbrothers?

And now a half sister?

Bob arrives a few minutes later. I climb in the front seat. As we drive away, Mercedes sits by herself, alone, still waiting.

"Is that a new friend?" Bob asks.

I shake my head. "Just a girl in my grade."

I'm quiet while Kenny talks to his dad about soccer practice from the back seat—ignoring my presence the whole time, of course. If there's no chessboard, he doesn't say anything to me. It's just as well. I know I'll keep quiet about Mercedes. There's no way I'm telling Bob or Kenny about Mercedes. I might not even tell my mom.

CHAPTER 8

Mercedes

The scrap of notebook paper is crushed at the bottom of my backpack. I pull it out and a corner rips. But I can still read the phone number. I smooth out the paper on my desk. Her sixes are lopsided, the bottom loop too big. Her sevens and ones look almost the same. I have to squint to see the little tail.

"Tristan! Mercedes!" Cristina calls from downstairs. About time. She was late to pick me up from school and then cooking took forever. I hear Tristan stampeding down for dinner like he's never eaten before, even though I gave him a Pop-Tart fifteen minutes ago when Cristina wasn't looking.

"Mercedes!" Cristina calls again. "Dinner!"

I try to remember the last time Mom made dinner. Or was home for dinner. Even when she isn't traveling, she almost always works late. When Mom first hired Cristina, I thought it would be weird to have some stranger living in my house, but having a nanny is better than the coming and going of babysitters.

"I made stir-fry." At least Cristina knows what I like to eat. The last time Mom was home, she ordered meat-lovers pizza. Gross. I don't eat animals.

"In a minute!" I yell back. "I'm in the bathroom."

To make it more true, I take my phone and the scrap of paper into my bathroom. Because you have to walk through my closet to get to my bathroom, Cristina is always telling me to put away my clothes so she doesn't trip on them when she comes to clean. I carefully step over the sneaker I left in the middle of the floor. *See?* I want to say to Cristina. *It's not that hard. You just work around whatever is in your way.*

I set the phone on the counter and pick up a brush. I watch myself brushing my hair, which just makes it frizzier. Like *hers.* I grab a hair tie from the pile next to the sink and yank my hair into a ponytail. Like hers. Sisters. Well, half sisters.

I pull out the ponytail, shake my hair loose, and enter the phone number—all those sixes and sevens. I don't really want to talk to her, but I have to make sure she'll keep my secret.

"Hello?" she answers on the second ring. Her voice is quiet, like it was when she first introduced herself. I should have texted. I almost hang up. "Hello?" she says again.

"Do you have a bike?"

"Who is this?" she asks.

I pull myself onto the bathroom counter and sit leaning against the mirror so I can't see my face—her face—anymore. "Mercedes. Your half sister." I spit out the words, trying to sound as annoyed as possible. The words feel weird in my mouth. "Do you have a bike?" I repeat.

"Um, yes."

Neither of us says anything.

"Why?"

"Do you know Laurel Park?" I ask. "Meet me there in thirty minutes."

"The park on the hill? I guess. Why?"

Ugh. She is so exasperating. "Can you meet me or not?"

"I'll have to ask my mom."

"Fine, go ask her." Cristina always lets me do whatever I want. And Mom's never home to decide one way or the other. "And then meet me there. Twenty minutes."

I hang up before she can say anything else. After I gulp down a plate of vegetable stir-fry, I grab my helmet from the back closet.

"Do you need any money?" Cristina asks as I buckle my helmet. Cristina has cash that's for me and Tristan. Kind of like allowance. Candy, new earrings, a yo-yo. Little things like that. We might not ever have Mom around, but we can buy just about anything we want.

"Sure," I say, and she hands me a twenty. Always take money when it's offered, that's my advice.

I get sweaty biking up the hill to Laurel Park. The wind whipping at my back feels good. It's just a little park with a swing set, a couple picnic tables, an enormous live oak tree. I bring Tristan here sometimes, although he prefers the bigger playgrounds—or the roller coasters and Speeding Saucers at the Boardwalk, if Cristina will take him. He loves adventure. He's like me that way.

Mattie's sitting on top of a picnic table when I arrive. I drop my bike next to hers and sit beside her.

"Matilde," I say because I can already tell it annoys her.

"Hi, Mercedes."

Silence.

Suddenly I'm not even sure why I wanted her to meet me.

She nervously snaps and unsnaps the buckle on her helmet. "What do you want?" she asks.

"I hope you didn't tell anyone. About us."

A look of panic or maybe pain shoots across her face. And then she looks away. I almost feel bad.

"I mean," I say, trying not to sound as cruel as I feel, "it's no one else's business, right?"

She shakes her head.

"Did you tell your mom?"

She shakes her head again. I'm so relieved, I almost smile.

"I just want to make sure you're not planning on telling everyone."

"You want me to keep this secret, is that it?" Mattie says, turning to look at me. Her eyes are wet and I'm afraid she's going to cry. "Because if that's it, fine. I'm going now." She spits out the words. I realize I'm not the only one who can get angry. "Is that all you wanted?"

I don't know what I want until I say it: "Tell me what you know."

"About what?" Like she doesn't know.

"Tell me what you know," I repeat. "You know, tell me the story you tell everyone."

She sighs. I can't help myself; I sigh, too.

"About Francisco Gómez?" She says his name so formally, I almost can't believe she's talking about the same person. Mom always called him Frank. *Frank lives in Colombia. Frank was too busy for one daughter, so I'm sure he's too busy for another one. Frank has his life; we have ours.*

Mattie jumps off the table and walks to the swing set. She

sits in a swing but doesn't pump her legs. "Well, I know he's my father."

"Ugh! I know that. We know that. We've established that." It's like she's trying to make me mad. I'm so annoyed, I consider getting back on my bike and spending my money at Starbucks. Instead, I reluctantly plop into the swing next to hers. Why did she have to show up at Poppy View Middle School? Why did she have to see that photo? Why did I think having her meet me here was a good idea? "That's seriously all you know?"

"Well, um, I know my parents met when he came to Minnesota for college. He and my mom got married. And then he kept going back to Colombia to do research or something. I think he had a sister who was sick a lot. Anyway." Mattie pauses. "He was never home and my mom didn't want to live in Colombia. When she got pregnant with me, she decided she didn't want to be married to someone who was never home." Mattie says all this like it's a script for a school play. She knows all the lines. She's probably said them a million times. I know what that's like. "They got divorced before I was born."

I take a deep breath and hold it.

"He went back to Colombia."

I exhale.

"And I've never met him," she says flatly.

"Me neither."

We don't look at each other, but we each kick off the dirt, letting our swings propel us back and forth.

CHAPTER 9

Mattie

✳

Mercedes is the one who demanded I meet her at Laurel Park and tell her everything I know, but now she's the silent one. A scrawny squirrel runs near us and then darts away, climbing the huge tree next to the swing set. Lucas showed me and my mom this park while Bob was busy with the movers. It's the closest playground to the house, but it's so small compared to the parks in the Saint Paul neighborhood I played in when I was his age. This one is just a slide and two swings. Mercedes and I swing back and forth on them now, neither of us speaking. I think of Mai, who never stops talking.

I told Mercedes that I haven't said anything to anyone about us, but that's not quite true. I called Mai and told her about my doppelgänger—or sister. Half sister. Whatever she is. Telling Mai made it a little more real to me, but I wish I could have told her the secret in person. FaceTiming isn't the same as seeing each other at school.

"A sister? A secret sister?" Mai said. Her eyes got huge and then crinkled in an excited giggle. "Okay, what if she knows your dad and then you get to meet him and then your parents get back together like in that one movie—"

I cut her off. "My mom just married *Bob*," I cried. "Even if

I ever *met* my dad, I'm sure they wouldn't get back together. I wouldn't want them to. My mom's happy now."

"But a sister!" Mai gushed again. "I know I complain about Houa and Eve, but I love having sisters."

Mai has a huge family—two sisters and four brothers—and lives with not only her parents but her grandma and aunt, too. Because she has such a big family, Mai takes care of her little brothers and sisters since she's the oldest girl. She also helps cook every night. Once a month her parents let her sleep over at my house.

"But you loved sleeping over at my house because it was quiet with no little sisters," I said to Mai.

Mai just laughed. "I like a little bit of quiet. But sisters are the best."

Mercedes twists back and forth in the playground swing. Having Mercedes as a sister—even a half sister—isn't looking like the best right now.

"Even if you haven't met him, at least you have his last name," Mercedes says accusingly. "Gómez."

"What difference does that make?"

"I have my mom's last name," Mercedes says. She's not looking at me.

"Miller?"

"That's what happens when your mom isn't married to your dad." Her voice is bitter like the white part of a slice of watermelon. "You're lucky your parents were married."

"Yeah, well, *you're* lucky you have the same last name as your mom," I tell her. "My mom *was* Valerie Gómez until she got remarried to my stepdad. Now she's Valerie Jasper. What a stupid name."

Mercedes sulks. I sulk. We say nothing.

"Now I'm the only Gómez." I stop my swing and think, *Except—*

"Except you're not the only Gómez," Mercedes interrupts my thoughts like a mind reader. "Frank Gómez. Mattie Gómez."

"So, you knew about me? You knew my mom was married to him? I mean," I pause, trying to find the right words, "I, um, didn't know anything about you."

Mercedes lets out a short laugh like a bark. "Obviously. You want to hear what I know?"

My phone pings just then. It's my mom:

When will you be home? Can you help Kenny with his math homework?

"I have to go pretty soon," I say.

"Listen," Mercedes says. She plants her feet so her swing stops moving. "You can go. It doesn't matter to me. I just thought you might want to know some stuff. Since you seem to know nothing. It's your life, too."

"Don't get like that, Mercedes." I sigh. She's so touchy. "Just tell me everything."

But she doesn't say anything at first. She jumps off the swings like she's going to leave. Instead, she paces and then circles the swing set. She's like a lion in a cage at the zoo.

Mercedes clears her throat and starts talking really fast. "Mom travels all over the world for her job, and she met him when she went to Bogotá. That's in Colombia, if you don't know. She was there for a few months. They were, like, boy-friend and girlfriend. He showed her this picture of a baby girl and said he was divorced. Anyway, they broke up, obviously. By the time she got back to San Francisco and realized she was pregnant with me, he was deep in the jungle—or maybe it's the mountains?"

Mercedes stops circling.

"As far as I know, he's been there ever since. She said he never even met the one daughter he did have, so there was no point in contacting him—even if it was possible to contact someone in the jungle."

"What was he doing in the jungle?"

"He's a famous anthropologist." She says this like it's the most obvious thing in the world.

"He studies dinosaurs?" I ask. Lucas is obsessed with dinosaurs. He has these little plastic figures and he knows the names of all of them even though he's only five. And he's constantly leaving them on the floor in the hallway, where we trip on them.

"How do you not know this? He's an anthropologist."

"Oh, wait," I say. "An archaeologist is the one that studies dinosaurs."

Mercedes groans. "No, archaeologists dig up human bones. You're thinking of a paleontologist."

I can feel my face get hot. Now Mercedes is going to think I'm so dumb. When, actually, I do know the differences between archaeologists and paleontologists. Goes to show that I've been spending too much time with a five-year-old boy. If my mom had never married Bob, none of this would be happening. I wouldn't have new stepbrothers. I would never have moved to California. And I never would have met Mercedes.

"He's not a paleontologist and he's not an archaeologist. He's an *anthropologist*. He studies, um . . ." She pauses. I realize that she might not know what an anthropologist does, either. "They study humans, not dig up bones," she says at last. "Like, culture, human behavior, that kind of thing. Anthropologists watch people, learn all about them by seeing what they do."

We watch a woman in track pants and a long-sleeved shirt that says *Run Like the Wind* jog through the park. Whenever I see someone jogging in their neon shoes and track clothes, I wonder if they're running toward something or away from something.

"That's his job?" I ask after the woman passes. "That's pretty cool. I knew he was in Colombia, but I didn't know about him being an anthropologist, him being in the jungle. Why do you think he's never come to meet us?"

Mercedes shrugs like she never really thought about it. "My mom said Frank Gómez couldn't handle having kids, what with living in the jungle all the time."

"My mom never said anything about him having another daughter. She must not know," I say. It's not a question, but I wish Mercedes could answer it.

Instead, she asks, "Does she ever talk to him?"

"Like on the phone?" I shake my head. "I remember that when I was little, she got a letter from him. That's it."

"Well, maybe he told her about Mom and me in that letter."

"She would have told me," I insist.

"Maybe she lied."

I think of how much my mom hates lies. When she lost her job, she told me, "You know I never liked that marketing job. There's so much dishonesty in advertising. And I hate lying to people—even little lies, even lies by omission. Lying is a terrible thing, Mattie. Each time you tell a lie, you lose a little part of yourself."

"She would never lie to me," I say to Mercedes.

I can tell Mercedes doesn't really believe that. I wonder who lies to her. I wonder who she lies to. She shrugs. "Then maybe she doesn't know."

"I can't believe it." I'm not sure which part I can't believe. That my father is a famous arc—I mean, anthropologist? That I have a half sister? That my mom never told me or never knew?

Mercedes buckles her helmet and climbs on her bike. But before she leaves, she turns and locks her eyes on mine. "Just because you've never heard a story before doesn't make it any less true."

As I coast down the hill from Laurel Park, I'm determined to ask my mom about everything Mercedes told me. I imagine what I'll say. I'll demand to know the truth. I might cry. My mom will tell me everything she knows. She has to. But after I put my bike away, I open the door and hear Kenny yelling, "You're not my mom!"

"Kenneth," Bob says in a stern, deep voice.

"She can't tell me what to do!"

I stay in the entryway, out of view of the living room. I hear Bob say, "Val may not be your mom—"

"Our mom died!" Kenny shouts. Usually it's Lucas shouting. Kenny is the quiet one. "You're not our mom!"

Now Lucas starts to cry.

Bob cuts them both off. "Yes, Mama is gone, but Val loves us. She's not trying to replace Mama, but she's here to help take care of you. And we all agree you need a shower, young man."

I shake my head. All this yelling over a shower?

Kenny starts whining again, but Bob interrupts him. "You're ten years old—old enough to know better, Kenny. Go take a shower."

Lucas stops crying long enough to shout proudly, "I had a bath already!"

There's no point in waiting any longer. I walk into the living room just in time to watch Kenny sulk toward the bathroom and Lucas dive-bomb his dad, who's on the couch next to my mom. "I'm clean! Smell me!" Lucas hollers. My mom's cup of tea spills on her lap and on his clean pajamas, and his tears begin all over again.

"How was the park?" she asks over the crying. She holds the dripping cup, sounding worn out, even though she's supposed to be a happy newlywed.

"He's tired," Bob says, as if we needed that explanation.

I feel like I'm interrupting the family evening, like this isn't my story.

"You still okay with helping Kenny with math? After his shower? And after he's calmed down?" She smiles weakly. "I tried to help with fractions, but you know my math skills."

"I know," I say.

"Bob's even worse."

"I can help."

We watch Bob carry a screaming Lucas off to bed.

"Can you also grab me a towel?" she asks, holding out

her mug. I know that while I help Kenny with fractions, she'll clean the kitchen. Then she and Bob will watch TV together while I finish my homework. Before we moved, my mom used to tuck me in and turn out my light every night. I still wish I could have a good-night kiss, the kind in the dark where you can smell your mom and feel her warm breath. Sometimes it's enough to feel something real without seeing it.

I bring her a towel and she gives me a grateful look. I know that because I don't cry or reject basic personal hygiene, I am a relief to her. And easy to overlook. She looked so happy when she was sorting photos and remembering the wedding. I decide to keep my questions—and my secrets—to myself. Not only because Mercedes told me to. The last thing my mom needs right now is me asking about some jungle dad.

CHAPTER 10

Mercedes

I jerk awake in the middle of the night to find Tristan standing next to my bed.

"Mermer," he whispers. He shifts back and forth on bare feet. "Are you awake?"

I reach for his hand. He has nightmares. When Mom's out of town—which is most of the time—he comes to me. Cristina's room is downstairs next to the kitchen, so she never hears him crying.

"I am now," I say, and sit up. "What was it about this time?"

Tristan sniffles. He better not be getting snot on my bedspread.

"There was a tornado and we all flew away."

"There are no tornadoes." I get out of bed. Every nightmare is different, but they're always about disasters. Cristina lets him watch too many movies. "Come on, I'll take you back to bed."

After I bring him a cup of water and he climbs under his covers, Tristan closes his eyes and smiles. "Thank you," he whispers. This is the one time having a brother isn't annoying.

Back in my own room, I can't get back to sleep. I get out of bed and look out the window at the trees of the neighborhood, the glimpse of rocky cliff, and the shadow of the ocean beyond.

The night sky is black, blank like a chalkboard before anyone has written on it. Then I spot one star hanging just above the water like the beginning of a story. We're learning about stars in science class and Ms. Garcia says that you can tell the stars apart from the planets because stars twinkle. The star balancing above the ocean twinkles. It winks at me. A strange, sticky feeling attaches itself to me like I was the one with the nightmare.

When I was eight, Mom took me to her great-aunt's funeral in Arizona. We stayed with Mom's only sister, Denise. One night I overheard Denise say to Mom, "She's going to start asking questions about her father, Jennifer. You can't just pretend she'll never want to know." But Mom just kept pretending.

I glare at the star winking at me. I want to know the story. The whole story. I *need* to know. And so does Mattie.

The next morning I head straight toward Mattie. I step between her and her locker. She's stuffing in an orange jacket that crinkles noisily. "Meet me back here at lunch," I hiss.

"What?" She turns around and I get a glimpse of yet another Minnesota fashion masterpiece. Her T-shirt is bright green and has a smiling snowman on it. It's seventy degrees in Santa Cruz today. Her socks are the same ridiculous bright green.

"If anyone asks," I say, "we're working on our mythology project."

When the bell rings for lunch, I tell Gaby and Rebecca to go ahead without me. "Ugh," I say. "I have to meet that weird new girl."

"Your twin?" Gaby teases. At least, I hope she's teasing and that she hasn't figured out my secret.

"Why?" Rebecca asks.

"Oh," I say as casually as I can, "something about our stupid mythology project."

This seems to satisfy my friends—they know how important good grades are to me.

I wait for them to turn the corner toward the lunchroom. Mattie is waiting for me by her locker, just like I told her to. She has her lunch bag in one hand and our social studies packet in the other. After the breezeway clears of other seventh graders, I join her.

"We have to find out more," I say.

"I agree. I think we should pick a different god."

"Mattie," I whisper. "Will you please just listen?"

"Aren't you talking about our social studies project?"

"No. We need to know more. About *him*."

At last I spot a flash of understanding on her face. "You mean what happened to our—to Francisco Gómez? But I told you everything I know."

"There must be more."

"You know more than me. I didn't even know he was an anthro-whatever."

"Haven't you ever tried to google him?" I ask her.

She shakes her head. "It never felt right. I mean, it's always been just me and my mom. The two of us." She pauses. "Well, it used to be."

"I have, and there are about a million Frank Gómezes in the world. Let me show you." I sit on the floor and pull out my phone. I type in **Frank Gómez**. She sits cross-legged beside me and looks at the screen. Wrestlers, school principals, accountants, high school students. The familiar list. None of them is my dad.

"Why don't you try Francisco instead of Frank?" Mattie asks.

"You don't think I haven't thought of that? Watch." I enter the words in the search box. More results. In Spanish. I don't want to admit to Mattie that I don't know a word of Spanish. But even if I could read Spanish, how would I ever find my dad in all these results? I feel my face getting hot. It's impossible.

"Have you tried his second last name?"

"What do you mean? Second last name?"

"Yeah, in Colombia, people have two last names. Their father's last name and their mother's last name. So, for example, my second name would be Hillman, which was my mom's last name. Mattie Gómez Hillman. If I were living in Colombia."

"Okay," I say, pretending like this isn't news to me. A second last name? Why didn't Mom ever tell me this? "So what's his second last name?"

Mattie looks at me. "I don't know. I thought you knew a bunch of stuff about him. That's pretty basic."

The angry feeling moves from my stomach up my arms. I really wish she would stop making me mad. If I let my hands do what they wanted to do, I would have pulled her hair at this point. I must remain calm. Cool. Collected.

"Well, think," I command. "There's got to be some way for us to figure out what it is. Did your mom ever mention any relatives? A grandmother?" Mattie shakes her head. "Neither did mine." What could his second last name be?

"I suppose you could try my middle name," Mattie says.

"Which is?"

"Flora. Matilde Flora Gómez."

What a name. "Okay, we'll try it." Instead of grabbing her ponytail, my fingers obediently tap. **Francisco Gomez.** Then I stop. We're both holding our breath. I slowly add *F-L-O-R-A* and then hit enter.

The screen rearranges itself.

Did you mean Francisco Gómez Flores?

"Yes!" I shout. "That's got to be it!"

"My mom must have taken the name Flores and changed it to Flora for my middle name," Mattie says.

As if I care about her middle name. All I care about is the results on the screen. Francisco Gómez Flores.

"Wait." Mattie grabs my phone before I can tap on the name. "What if he's—" She pauses. "Dead?"

Dead? There's no way Frank Gómez can be dead. In his picture, he looks so healthy. *But what if?* I wonder.

"What if he was eaten by a tiger?" I can't help asking.

"Do they have tigers in Colombia?"

"Not a tiger. What do they have there? A mountain lion?"

"I think they have jaguars. That's the one with spots, right?" Mattie bites her upper lip. "But someone would have told us if that had happened."

I nod and think out loud. "Maybe he hunts for treasures like in *Tomb Raider* and he got caught?"

"What if he was kidnapped?" she says. Then she whispers, "People used to get kidnapped in Colombia all the time. And there are earthquakes. My mom said that's why we could never go there."

Maybe that's why Mom always insisted: *No, I'm never going*

back to Colombia. Was she afraid of getting kidnapped? Afraid of earthquakes? I shake my head. No, Mom isn't afraid of anything.

"Why do they call it kidnapping when it happens to adults?" Mattie asks.

"Mattie," I say, "focus."

She shrugs. "What if—"

Two sixth-grade boys turn the corner and walk toward us. I glare at them and they scurry away.

Mattie tries again. "What if he has a new family? What if he married some . . ." Her face darkens. "I don't know, a French woman, and now he lives in France and eats cheese?"

Eats cheese? I shake my head at her. She's so weird. "Maybe he hit his head during one of his expeditions into the jungle and has amnesia." I picture tall trees and jungle vines and coconuts. "And now he doesn't remember us or our moms. Or even his own name."

"Like in a TV show?"

I sigh. "I guess that's not very likely." Francisco Gómez's disappearance probably isn't because of something interesting or exciting or even dangerous. He probably just never wanted to be found. Never wanted to meet either of his daughters. I want there to be a good reason neither of us has ever met him. But there probably isn't.

Maybe Mattie has been thinking the same thing because her shoulders slump. "What if he works in a super-boring office job in some boring city and is ashamed that he's not a famous archaeologist anymore?"

"Anthropologist," I correct, and snatch my phone back from her. And tap the name of our father.

Mattie

❋

rancisco Gómez Flores is not dead. Sitting on the floor in the breezeway during lunch, Mercedes and I scroll through all the search results on her phone. It's clear that he's not married to a cheese-eating French woman. He doesn't have a boring office job. It seems unlikely that he was ever kidnapped. What is obvious is that Francisco Gómez Flores is most definitely an anthropologist.

"Look at that," Mercedes says and then she whistles that way people do when something is amazing. I can't whistle at all. If I could, right now I would, because what we're looking at *is* amazing. On the screen in front of us is a whole page of important-sounding websites and articles, pictures, and diagrams, all about or by Francisco Gómez Flores.

Mercedes navigates over to the images tab and that's when we see it. A photo. A photo of a man wearing a khaki vest full of pockets standing on a steep mountainside.

"It's him," she says.

Mercedes clicks on the picture. It fills up the whole screen. Below the image, the caption reads *Francisco Gómez Flores, June 7.*

"That was taken this summer," I murmur. I try to remember what I might have been doing the day that photo was taken. The day my father stood on that mountain. I think back. School had been out for a week, maybe. I was probably riding my bike with Mai, probably going to buy ice cream cones. It was after I knew my mom was getting married and we were moving to California, but before I really understood that I would have a new life and a new family.

Now I swat away the thought. I push away the memory of that June day getting ice cream cones with Mai and how much I miss my best friend. I push the delete key on the memories and hold it down until they disappear. I concentrate only on the screen. This man. My father.

Mercedes scrolls through one page after another; all the results are images and articles about Francisco Gómez Flores. She clicks the links, some in indecipherable Spanish and some in equally foreign-sounding English.

Indigenous populations and shamanism. Ecodevelopment in Guaviare. Indigenizing methodologies of South American field research. Conceptual reflections of origin mythologies. El ecodesarrollo en regiones indígenas. Investigación de antropológica. La mitología de las culturas indígenas de las montañas.

"Do you understand Spanish?" I ask Mercedes, secretly hoping she doesn't. My mom thinks it's funny that I'm half Colombian but can hardly ask where the baño is. I say it's her fault for not teaching me. When people see my last name, they always ask if I speak Spanish. Or worse: they start talking to me in Spanish and then I just stand there looking dumb.

"Do you?" Mercedes stops scrolling and looks at me, her eyes—my eyes—boring into me. I shake my head. She breaks our stare. "Me neither."

And still we click and scroll. Spanish, English. Every article mentions Colombia. *Santa Marta. Bogotá. Tayrona. Boyacá.* Once my mom showed me a magazine featuring photos of Colombia. There were steep green mountains and white beaches. Aqua-blue water and palm trees. Slinking rivers through dense rain forest. "This is where your dad lives," she had said. "Beautiful, isn't it?" It was one of the only times she talked about Colombia.

Scroll and click. Our foreheads are nearly touching; her flyaways tickle my cheek. I have no idea what we're looking for. *Comparative mythology in pre-Columbian societies. Sociopolitical structures of Aracataca peoples. Dichotomy of Indigenous philosophies.*

None of the articles are very interesting looking.

Mercedes scrolls back to the first photo and clicks the link beside it. There's a short article, just a paragraph below the photo. We both read.

Dr. Francisco Gómez, the esteemed cultural anthropologist and ethnographer from Bogotá, Colombia, will be joining the faculty as this year's Dupree Visiting Professor at Northern Madrone College for a semester of teaching and scholarship. We are fortunate to have Dr. Gómez, who is taking a break from his years-long immersion in Sierra Nevada de Santa Marta, to teach two upper-level courses that will provide students in Northern Madrone's esteemed anthropology department with a fresh perspective on cultural anthropology fieldwork in South America.

Mercedes turns into a statue. Her phone slips from her fingers.

"What is it?"

She doesn't move.

"What's the matter?"

"Northern Madrone College." She doesn't look at me, just says the words slowly, carefully, one at a time.

"Weird, isn't it? That doesn't sound like Colombia."

She shakes her head but doesn't say anything. The bell rings to mark the end of lunch. "It's not in Colombia," she says. "It's here. In California. I've been there."

Now it's my turn to freeze like the Minnesota snowman on my shirt. It can't be true. He's supposed to be in Colombia. I imagine him in the button-down shirt and neat haircut he wears in the photo I have of him. I feel dizzy, like gravity isn't quite holding me down.

Francisco Gómez—my father—is here in California?

CHAPTER 12

Mercedes

n less time than it takes for the breezeway to fill with students, I've already decided. I'm going to Northern Madrone College to find Frank Gómez.

And Mattie is coming with me.

"It doesn't make sense," she says, as lockers bang and kids shout.

I'm on my feet and I pull Mattie up.

"Mattie," I say, squeezing her arm.

"Ow!" she cries.

"It's a sign." Last summer I had a regional cross-country meet at Northern Madrone College. It was supposed to be in June, but it got rescheduled to July and Mom was off to Tokyo by then. Instead, Cristina drove me. I was probably the only runner in the history of middle school sports who didn't have a parent cheering from the bleachers. Cristina cheered, but she's paid to do stuff like that. I try to remember if I noticed anyone who looked like he could have been my father. Was Frank Gómez there that day? What if I actually did have a parent there, but I didn't know it?

"But—" Mattie rubs her arm, even though I barely touched her. Wow, you can really tell she's not used to having siblings.

She would never survive the grabbing and pinching me and Tristan do when we're mad at each other.

"There's got to be a bus. I bet there's one we can catch today. Or tomorrow! We'll take the Santa Cruz Transit bus to the campus—I'm pretty sure it goes to all the way to the college." *Or maybe the bus only goes to UC Santa Cruz?* I think to myself. "Whatever," I say aloud. "We'll just hop on and—"

"No," she interrupts. She fiddles with her locker and swings it open, stuffing her uneaten lunch inside.

"But—"

"I'm not saying no to this harebrained idea, but I'm not saying yes, either. I will say that I'm only going if we make a plan."

I let out an exasperated sigh. Fine. "Fine, you win. We'll make a plan. Come over to my house tonight—"

"I can't tonight."

"Mercedes!" I turn around and Gaby and Rebecca are running toward me. They're both waving and laughing. Perfect timing.

I look from Mattie to my two best friends. Whenever I'm invited to either of their houses for big holidays (Rosh Hashanah for Rebecca and a big Mexican Christmas for Gaby), I feel like a scientist learning about a strange civilization. Rebecca's family is so perfect—she's best friends with her older brother, Noah (who Gaby has a crush on) and her parents kiss in front of them. Ew! Gaby has a stay-at-home mom, who makes the best chilaquiles and lets us stay up all night during sleepovers. Even though they know about how I have a single mom and a brother who doesn't look like me, I can tell they don't really understand. They always talk about Tristan's dad as if he were *my* dad. They don't get it that people can be siblings and not have the same dad.

"Mercedes!" they shout again, getting nearer.

"Look," I say to Mattie. "We need to figure this"—I wave my hand between her and me and back to her—"whole thing out. And you're the one who wants a plan." I sigh as dramatically as I can. "How about Friday?"

She nods.

I lower my voice. Gaby and Rebecca are almost here. "And remember. Do *not* tell your mom. There's no need to get anyone—especially moms—involved right now."

"What will I tell her, then?"

"What are you doing?" calls Rebecca.

"You never came to lunch!" says Gaby.

I glance up and give them a big juicy smile like nothing is different, like nothing has changed. "Hey!" I yell as cheerily as possible. I whip around and whisper to Mattie. "Just tell your mom we're working on our social studies project at your new friend's house on Friday." Letting Mattie come over will be worth it if she can help me. "But don't tell anyone else anything!"

Just then Rebecca reaches me, grabbing my hand and pulling me toward art class. I hiss in Mattie's ear, "I'll text you my address. See you on Friday."

"All right, I got it, Mercedes." Now *she* sounds annoyed. Which makes me even more annoyed.

CHAPTER 13

Mattie

Not what we usually do on a school night," my mom says after school, "but definitely better than cooking dinner and doing dishes." Her new wedding ring glints as she climbs in the passenger seat of the minivan. She winks at Bob, who's got his hands on the steering wheel. "I could get used to life in California."

"Yay!" shouts Lucas from the last row in the minivan.

Even though it's a school night, the Jasper family is going out. Back home in Minnesota, we never went anywhere on weeknights. My mom came home from work at five, I helped her make dinner, and then I did my homework while she watched the news. Sometimes we played a game on her phone or I helped her with a crossword puzzle—usually her figuring out the answers and me writing the letters in the little boxes. On Thursdays I got to stay up later than usual and watch TV. As long as my homework was done, she let me curl up on the couch with her. In the winter she would drink tea and I would have a hot chocolate. In the summer we made her special drink, mint fizz, which was just a few leaves of mint from her pot on the step mixed with sparkling water. This, though, is a totally different Thursday.

"You'll love the Boardwalk, Mattie," Bob says as he pulls out of the driveway.

"Roller coaster!" shouts Lucas.

"Can I get a corn dog? And an ice cream cone?" Kenny asks.

I expect my mom to say that corn dogs aren't dinner, but she just laughs.

When we arrive, the boys shoot out of the car like a cannon. They're excited about the rides, but I don't like speed or heights—in other words, I hate roller coasters. I like knowing what's going to happen next, not being surprised by bumps and drops.

"Can I get cotton candy?" I ask my mom when I see a concession stand, even though I know my super-health-crazy mom will never let me.

"I suppose," she says. "Sounds like we'll just have a junk food dinner."

I stare at her. What has happened to my mother?

"Ready for the roller coaster, Mattie?" Bob asks after our questionable dinner—lots of hot dogs and ice cream and fries.

"Mattie hates fast," my mom says.

"I like slower things," I say. "Like chess." I glance at Kenny, hoping maybe he'll acknowledge my existence. But he just says, "I love roller coasters. Especially this one. It's extra fast."

"Sounds exciting to me," my mom says.

"A little adventure never hurt anyone," Bob says, gripping my mom's hand and grinning. "Right, Kenny?" When Bob smiles at Kenny, the skin around the edges of his eyes crinkles like old aluminum foil.

The roller coaster, made of wooden boards painted white, looms over everything. It does not look sturdy enough for

Kenny, much less Bob. It makes me nervous just looking at it. I follow a few steps behind the four straggly people who make up my new family. Kenny sticks a finger up his nose. Lucas picks up a lollipop off the ground and licks it. Bob sneaks a kiss on my mom's neck. They're all gross.

"Do I have to go?" I ask my mom.

"I wanna ride the Speeding Saucers!" shouts Lucas, his mouth blue from the used lollipop.

"Would you rather take Lucas on his ride instead?" my mom asks.

Hmmm . . . a terrifying high-speed stomach drop or a little-kid ride? Not a tough choice. "I'll take Lucas," I gladly volunteer.

"Okay, great, honey," my mom says. I can tell she thinks this is proof that our new family is working out perfectly. "We'll meet you back at the Speeding Saucers," she calls as she follows Bob and Kenny toward the dangers of the roller coaster.

"Ready?" I ask Lucas.

"Let's go!"

The Speeding Saucers ride is a bunch of seats in these things that are painted to look like spaceships that spin around in different directions. It's one of the rides I actually don't mind.

"Pick a ship, Lucas," I say after we give the ride operator our tickets. Lucas runs to one that's painted with orange and red flames. The man who took our tickets comes around and pulls the safety bar down over our laps. Lucas squeezes in close to me. His warm little body smells like grease and ketchup and blue raspberry. The ride starts slowly at first, the whirring of the engine echoing in my ears.

"Fun!"

"It hasn't even really started yet," I tell him. "Just wait."

Pretty soon the saucers are rotating. The whole ride goes around in circles, spinning even faster. "Wheeee!" Lucas shouts and scoots closer to me. "This is SO fun, Mattie!"

We spin backward. The ride picks up speed. Around and around we go, like planets in orbit, swirling and twirling. The force of the turns pushes his little five-year-old body toward me. Lucas grabs my arm and whoops. My new world whips past: first the dark-green Santa Cruz Mountains, then the sparkly Pacific Ocean. We whirl around in pointless circles, laughing and shouting. I haven't felt this free since we moved here. Maybe having a little brother isn't going to be so bad, I think. That is, until we get off.

"That was fun, wasn't it?" I ask as we wind our way through the gates to the exit. Lucas doesn't answer. "Lucas?" I look down at him. I don't know my new stepbrother very well, but I do know he should be shouting and excited right now. Instead, his pale skin is even whiter than usual—almost green. He clutches his stomach.

I crouch next to him. He starts to cry. "Are you okay—"

And that's when half-digested corn dog and ice cream gushes in a torrent onto my shoes. Lucas moans. He tries to bury his face in my lap and then retches again. I fall on the cement with a thud. My stomach bounces. No! This is so disgusting and embarrassing. How did I ever think having a little brother would be a good thing? I just hope no one I know sees me like this.

"Oh, no, you two!" My mom appears just then and rushes toward me, dropping Bob's hand. Kenny, who holds a gigantic funnel cake, follows. "What happened?" she asks, even though it's obvious. "I'm sorry, Mattie."

"Too much of a good thing, Luke?" Bob asks, kneeling next to his crying kid.

I feel like crying, too. But when I look up at my mom, I realize she and Bob are trying not to laugh. She pulls a couple flimsy paper napkins from her purse and hands one to Bob and one to me. I wipe away the warm puke from my jeans, but they're probably ruined. I watch my mom help Bob clean up this little boy. My mom, being a mother to this stranger. Kenny stands to the side like he's embarrassed to be seen with us. Which is fair.

Then Lucas scrambles to his feet, wipes his mouth on the clean edge of his T-shirt. He hugs his dad. "I feel a lot better now!" He runs back and forth, twirling in circles as if nothing happened. "That was awesome, Mattie!"

That was about as far from awesome as it could be. A surge of something—anger or frustration or humiliation—swirls from my toes, up my legs, out my arms, and into my fingers. I scramble to my feet and ball the gross napkins. Tears prick my eyes. Kenny shuffles toward me and, without a word, grabs the napkins from my hands and throws the mess in a trash can. I open my mouth to say thanks, but before I can say anything, my mom puts an arm around my shoulder. "I'm so sorry, Mattie-mouse."

I look around the Boardwalk. I don't see anyone I recognize from school. This is the first time since we moved to California that I'm glad I don't know anyone.

CHAPTER 14

Mercedes

There she is. Mattie Gómez at the Boardwalk. I didn't think she knew that kids from Poppy View Middle School hang out at the Boardwalk on Thursday nights. Every week until the Boardwalk closes for the winter, it's a tradition to eat junk food, ride the scariest rides, and look for people we know.

"Isn't that—" I say to Gaby and Rebecca. I'm about to point out Mattie when I realize she's with her family. A woman with long ash-brown hair and glasses is holding hands with a gray-haired guy in a blue polo shirt. There are two boys, too. One of them looks to be about Tristan's age. They're heading toward the roller coaster, the older boy leading the way.

"Who?" Rebecca asks.

There's something private about seeing Mattie with her family. "Never mind," I say.

"Come on, Mercedes, let's go to the arcade." Gaby pulls me along, our matching bracelets clanging.

I've convinced my friends that the arcade is the best part of the Boardwalk. That way, I never have to admit that I hate rides. I just don't like the feeling of being out of control. Besides, it's a good place for them to spot boys from school.

Gaby and Rebecca are starting to get "boy crazy," as Cristina calls it. I don't really care, personally. Boys can be cool and they can be dorks, just like everyone else.

"Look, there's Joaquin at the Super Dance Shuffle!" Rebecca, who has a huge crush on Joaquin, says.

Her crush means she has to follow him and that means Gaby and I have to follow her. I don't mind because I'm a champion at the Dance Shuffle. When I play, I always get a crowd around me. The more people watching, the better I do.

Tonight is no different. I jump on the blue and red squares and obey every pattern the Shuffle gives me. My hips are swaying, my hair is bouncing. People are clapping and I'm laughing. I end up beating Joaquin by fifty points.

"Why did you have to do that?" Rebecca whines. After Joaquin lost, he stomped off toward the beach with his friends.

"Who cares?" I say, slinging an arm over her shoulder. "Forget about the stupid boys. And anyway, it's time to go meet your dad."

We walk toward the other end of the Boardwalk for our ride home. Some older kids goof around but most of the families have gone home. Except one.

We're almost at the Speeding Saucers (Tristan's favorite ride) when I spot Mattie's family again. Her parents are still holding hands. Gross. And the older boy is eating a funnel cake. Where's the little one and where's Mattie?

That's when I see it. It's like slow motion. A slow-motion horror movie. Mattie walks out of the Speeding Saucers ride with the little boy. He stops walking and she crouches down. And then, before anyone can do anything, the boy is puking all over. It's a disgusting mess of chunky yellow and brown. Mattie's jeans are covered in the stuff. Even from where we stand, I can smell the vomit. I gag. I don't know how Mattie survived. If that were me, there would have been a puke fest. At least she'll be cleaned up before she comes over tomorrow. Her parents come running, but I can tell they're trying not to laugh.

Just like Gaby and Rebecca. Except they're not trying not to. They're laughing. I yank them behind a stand that sells souvenir hats so Mattie doesn't see us.

"OMG!" Gaby shrieks. "That's the new girl. The one who looks like you! Gross!"

"Mercedes, look!" Rebecca squeezes my arm. She's giggling along with Gaby. "That is so disgusting!"

I let out a halfway laugh. "Ew! Let's go this way so we don't have to see that." I point my friends toward the parking lot.

"Remember when Peter Han threw up in third grade?" Rebecca says, spotting her dad and waving.

Gaby laughs. "What ever happened to Puking Pete?"

I watch Mattie for one second longer. She doesn't see me.

"I almost feel sorry for her," Gaby says after we tell Rebecca's dad what happened.

I nod and laugh with them. But I *do* feel sorry for her. I don't want her to become another middle school story. And I *definitely* do not want anyone finding out who she is.

CHAPTER 15

Mattie

Even though hanging out with Mercedes Miller on Friday night after my first week in a new school is pretty much the last thing I want to do right now, at least the week is over. Getting caught up with assignments, figuring out where to go for each class, and trying to make new friends is exhausting. I miss Mai so much, especially at lunch. In the cafeteria today, I caught Gaby and Rebecca staring at me and laughing, but Mercedes shushed them with a scowl every time. I guess I'm not even worth her laugh.

"Don't pay attention to them," Sunny whispered, giving me a shy smile. I'm glad to have her and November and Ted to sit with.

When Bob pulls up at the address Mercedes gave me, Lucas shouts from the back seat, "Wow, it's a mansion!" He's right. Mercedes's house definitely looks like a mansion. It's tall and square like a Lego building. Huge windows face the ocean. Round shrubs dot the walkway to a tiled front step. After I ring the doorbell, I wave to my mom, who's in the passenger seat. They're taking Lucas and Kenny to a movie while I'm here.

"Come on," Mercedes says, opening the front door.

I enter and my eyes bulge as I take in the two-story

entryway. It's all white marble, and the railing at the top of the stairs is like a balcony for Romeo and Juliet. Mercedes's life must be so perfect. I pull off my dirty sneakers but don't let go of my backpack—or its precious cargo. Mercedes leads me into the all-white living room. The walls, carpet, and furniture are white. The orange light from the sunset over the ocean is the only color. At the other end of the expanse of white carpeting, I catch a glimpse of a gigantic, gleaming white kitchen. Everything matches, just like Mercedes's clothes match her nails and the way her shoes are coordinated with her friends' shoes.

"Wow." I don't know what else to say.

"It's my mom's stuff," she says, and shrugs. "My mom's idea to live here."

"Where's your mom?"

"Tokyo."

"The one in Japan?"

Mercedes just shrugs. On a table beside the sofa is an ornate black enamel clock with gold dragons. It goes *tick, tick.* The sun dips below the water, and the big windows turn into mirrors. I watch myself fidget. Mercedes's reflection smooths her hair. From the kitchen, I hear a small voice that reminds me of Lucas. A refrigerator door opens and closes; a microwave roars to life. I hear the snapping of popcorn popping. The voice shifts from mumbled words to giggling shrieks.

Mercedes rolls her eyes. "What's going on in there?" she yells.

A pretty young woman in an oversized sweatshirt and leggings comes out of the kitchen. "Oh, Mercedes," she says, "I didn't realize you had a friend here."

Mercedes shrugs at the word "friend" and says, "This is Mattie."

"I'm the nanny," the woman says. "Cristina."

Mercedes rolls her eyes again. It must give her a headache—all the eye rolling. "Cristina is my *brother's* nanny," she clarifies.

"Their mom travels a lot," Cristina says. "She's been gone since . . ." She looks at Mercedes, who does not look back. "She's been gone since July, but she's coming home in time for Thanksgiving." She smiles. Mercedes does not.

Not home until Thanksgiving? I think of my mom. The longest she's been away was the four days she came to California last spring when Bob proposed. I can't imagine not seeing her for months.

"We'll be in my room. Can you get us a snack?" Mercedes asks. Actually, she doesn't really ask, she demands.

Cristina returns with a tray piled with packages of fruit snacks and bags of chips. A few bottles of assorted beverages are tucked under her arm. Imagine living here, with this life.

"Tell Tristan not to bug us." Mercedes takes the snacks from the nanny without a thank-you.

She doesn't wait for me, either. I scurry to follow her up the stairs, taking them as fast as I can. My supplies rattle in my backpack. I catch up with Mercedes in an upstairs hallway lined with brightly colored paintings in gold frames. There are narrow tables with lumpy sculptures made of rough stone. Little nooks in the wall hold ancient-looking pottery bowls. Mercedes waves a hand at the art. "More of my mom's show-off junk," she says. "Come this way."

We turn and I follow her into a room that's the size of at

least four of my bedrooms. Like the living room, it also has big windows that are black mirrors in the dark. Each of the three walls are painted a different color: pink, orange, green. Mercedes plops down on one of two beanbags that face the windows.

I drop my backpack on the floor by the other beanbag, but I don't sit down. Her room is like a museum. A half-sister museum. My mom and I always had a once-a-month museum visit. We would pick a different one each time. Art museums, science museums, fishing museums. I wonder if we'll still have museum day and if we'll have to bring Kenny and Lucas. Mercedes's museum has posters of movies and bands I've heard of but know nothing about. Competing with the posters are more gold-framed paintings of landscapes and night skies and abstract rectangles—obviously more of her mom's "junk."

"Do you ever go visit your mom when she's traveling? Have you been to Tokyo?"

"No," she says with a shrug. She inspects her fingernails and picks at the sparkly silver polish. A crumb of silver lands on the white carpet. "It's cool, though. Cristina lets me do whatever I want, so I barely even notice my mom is gone."

Imagine this life, I think again. But this time, I almost feel sorry for her.

I wander over to a big unmade bed buried in coordinated pillows. Next to it is a table piled with magazines and bottles of nail polish in an array of Mercedes-type colors. Juicy Tangerine, Spring Bloom, Beaming Sun. In another corner is a desk with a laptop, printer, and a stack of the same textbooks I have at home. On top of the printer is the pink binder. Francisco

Gómez's face looks back at me from beneath the plastic cover.

"Does your mom ever talk about him?" I ask, finally sliding into the beanbag next to her.

She shakes her head. "Does yours? My mom acts like he never even existed. It's like she doesn't realize I've had sex ed and I know that there has to be some kind of dad. I mean, I know I came from somewhere." Mercedes is clenching and unclenching her hands into fists in her lap.

"Me too. My mom just changes the subject anytime I ask about him."

"Mine, too. Does your mom turn off TV shows and movies about dads?"

"My mom didn't like *Beauty and the Beast* because of the nice dad."

Mercedes laughs. "My mom *hated* Maurice!"

"Mine didn't like *The Lion King* because of the dad." Before I met Mercedes, I hardly thought about him. But now I want—*need*—to find him. He's like the gravitational pull between the Earth and moon that Ms. Garcia talked about.

"I bet Frank Gómez likes Mufasa," Mercedes says.

We smile at each other briefly—like maybe we're in this together.

Wait until she sees what's in my backpack.

CHAPTER 16

Mercedes

I cannot believe what's in Mattie's backpack. There, at my feet, I see: a tattered bus schedule with brown stains, a faded map of Santa Cruz, a packet of wipes and a bottle of hand sanitizer, a box—an entire box!—of tissues, her school ID with her goofy smile, a baby picture, a complete change of clothes all the way down to the flowered underwear, a noisy orange plastic rain jacket, a rainbow-striped water bottle, a pocket knife, a first aid kit, and a flashlight.

"May I present," Mattie says with a flourish of her hand, "Operation D.A.D."

"Operation what?" I ask. *This girl.* "Have you gone completely bonkers?"

"No, Mercedes, I'm just a good planner. We want to find Francisco Gómez, right? We don't want anything to go wrong. So," she says, smiling proudly, "Operation D.A.D. Otherwise known as Operation Dare to Activate your Dreams."

"You're kidding, right?"

She's not kidding. "Do you like Operation Dads Are Dynamite better?"

"More like Operation Don't Act Dumb."

"Operation Definitely Act Defiant?"

We're laughing now, but Mattie tries to be serious.

"I'm serious," she says. "I've thought of everything. I hope you have some money for bus fare." She holds up the wipes. "See? We can sanitize anything we have to touch, like bus seats. And if we have to sneeze, we have tissues. My mom didn't have any smaller packages, sorry."

"What do we need an old map and bus schedule for?"

"To find our way, obviously."

I hold up my phone. "Haven't you ever used Maps on your phone?" I nudge the flashlight with my toe. "And, I don't know about you, but my phone has a flashlight, too."

"Okay, fine, we don't need those." Mattie shoves the flashlight, map, and transit schedule back into her bag. "But we definitely need these." She holds up her ID and baby picture.

I grab the picture. There is little chubby Mattie with round cheeks, thick black hair, and her tongue sticking out. Mom told me that when she first started dating Frank Gómez, he showed her a photo of his baby that he had never met. I always imagined his daughter as a baby—like in this picture. When I thought about Frank's daughter, I never imagined her growing up, just like me. I look from the picture to the girl in front of me to try to see if I can tell she's the same person. I wonder if Mom would recognize Mattie from the photo she saw.

"This is how we'll prove who we are when . . ." She pauses. "When we find our dad."

"Okay, I guess that's a good idea. But I don't think we need to worry about clean underwear."

"What if the bus breaks down? Or what if there's a mudslide and we can't make it home?"

I roll my eyes. "In that case, you forgot about toothbrushes."

"You're right!" Mattie takes out a gold-trimmed notebook. She opens it to a page covered in scribbles and I watch her write *Toothbrush and toothpaste.*

"What's the knife for, killer?" I ask.

"If we get lost, we can leave behind hashmarks on tree trunks to mark the way."

"You do know we're going to a college, not the Alaskan wilderness, don't you?"

Mattie picks up her knife. "I took it—I mean, *borrowed* it—from Kenny," she says.

"Who's Kenny?"

"My mom's new husband's kid."

"In other words, your stepbrother?"

She shrugs.

"Well, you can let him keep it. I don't think we'll be slashing up trees."

"We could use it for self-defense?"

I hold up my phone again. "9-1-1 is my self-defense. And my camera. You always have to video record everything."

"Fine," Mattie says. "But you have to admit we need this." She opens the first aid kit. It's stocked with Band-Aids and antiseptic and little packets of Tylenol.

"Fine," I say, with the same attitude as hers. "Keep it." While Mattie sorts her supplies, I open the transit app on my phone. I've taken the bus to the mall a couple times with Gaby, who knows all about the buses. But I've never done it by myself. "We'll go next Friday after school," I tell Mattie. I don't explain that that's Tristan weekend to go to his dad's. That it will be easier for me to leave if I don't have to worry about my brother.

I scan through the schedules and the maps. "Bad news, Mattie," I say at last. "Transit doesn't go all the way to Northern Madrone College. We can get about halfway there." I lean over and show her the map. She grabs the phone from my hands.

"What?" Panic flashes across her face. "That's terrible! What are we going to do?" She scrolls around on the app. And then she sighs. "No, Mercedes, look. We'll just have to switch buses. See?"

I grab my phone back. She's right. We'll have to transfer. No problem. I've heard people asking for transfers. We'll be able to do it. I hope.

"My mom's coming to pick me up in ten minutes. And we're not even close to ready."

"Just tell her you need to stay later. You can sleep over if you want." I gesture at the backpack. "You have plenty of stuff."

"But I don't have my toothbrush, remember?"

"I have extras. Besides, haven't you ever skipped a night?"

"I guess." Mattie looks unsure. She digs in her backpack again and pulls out her phone. She doesn't say anything, just scrolls. I catch a glimpse of her photos. Pictures of her smiling with other kids. "I haven't had a sleepover since July. Me and my friend Mai."

She sounds sad and I want to shove her sadness away. "Look," I snap, "it doesn't matter to me what you do. Just decide."

"Are you sure?"

I'm not sure I want Mattie Gómez sleeping over, no. On

the other hand, she *is* my half sister. Maybe it'll be okay.

"Thanks." After some tapping on her phone, she says, "Hello? How was the movie?" There's a pause. "I was wondering if I can stay overnight." Another pause. "Yes, her nanny is here. It's fine with her." Mattie looks at me as if to say, *Is it?* I nod. "It's the same number. You can call her. Okay, I will. I promise. I love you."

"Here," I say when she tosses aside her phone. "Have an iced tea." I throw her the bottle.

Once we've devoured half the snacks, we divide the job of planning our escape—and our exit strategy. She studies the campus map and I look through the bus schedules.

"You take the 1-A bus to Davenport," I say, "and then you transfer to the 7."

"Let me see," Mattie says, grabbing my phone. "No, you have to transfer to the 6."

"Give it back!" I reach for my phone, but she holds it out of reach. "You're getting chip dust all over it."

"Oh, never mind," Mattie says, tossing back my phone. "You're right. We catch the 7."

I *harrumph* and turn away. She's so annoying.

"I don't know, Mercedes," she says after we've been silently studying our plans for a few minutes. "Should we really do this?"

"Don't be a scaredy-cat!"

"But maybe—"

"Matilde," I say sharply. "We're either doing this or we're not doing it. Are you doing it?"

Mattie doesn't look at me. She stands and tears open her fourth package of fruit snacks.

"Look, if something goes wrong, we'll call Cristina, take an Uber," I say when she doesn't answer.

"Well, as long as we have a backup plan," Mattie mumbles at last. I don't think she's totally convinced, but at least she's going along with my plan—and writing it all down in her notebook. She finishes it just before one o'clock in the morning. From a sleeping bag on the floor, she reads the Operation D.A.D. plan aloud.

"Next Friday, Mattie and Mercedes (hereafter known as M & M) will get permission to go to the library after school."

Mattie insisted on having a very specific plan to sneak away.

"Instead of going to the library, M & M (the girls, not the candy) . . ."

Our fourth argument was about the initials. I thought it made us sound like candy, so Mattie added that last part.

"M & M will catch the 305 Santa Cruz Transit 1-A bus to Pacific Avenue. They will disembark and catch the transfer at 3:48. If they miss that one, there's another one at 4:18."

Mattie got worried that we might miss the bus, so we had to add that to the plan.

"They will ride the bus (after cleaning the seats with wipes) until they arrive at Northern Madrone Way. They will then walk the half mile to the college campus."

Mattie freaked out when she realized we'll have to walk. The girl must not get much exercise. I told her a half mile is nothing.

"M & M will consult the campus map (online and printed) to find the Humanities Building, where they will find the anthropology department and meet their dad, Francisco Gómez Flores."

It sounds so easy.

She yawns. *"Mercedes will pay for the bus fare,"* she concludes. "Did I get everything?"

My eyes are already closed. "Yes, everything."

Next week can't get here soon enough.

CHAPTER 17

Mattie

B ig news, class," Ms. Garcia says on Monday. She always wears precisely coordinated clothing—red sweater with black pants and red shoes or blue dress with blue high heels and blue earrings. Today she's wearing lemon-yellow heels and a daisy-patterned dress. Despite her cheery outfits, she hasn't smiled once during my whole first week at Poppy View Middle School. But today she does. "Field trip for the seventh grade coming up this Friday," she says, passing around pink paper.

While I wait for the permission slips to come around, I think about Mercedes and our mission. The more I thought about going to find Francisco Gómez, the more it seemed like a bad idea. I wouldn't dare tell Mercedes this, but I'm worried it won't work. Even with my supplies, my Operation D.A.D. plans, and Mercedes's allowance, I'm not sure. How will we find the right bus? The transfer? What about the walk to the campus? Even though we had talked through it all, I wasn't ready to leave when Bob picked me up from Mercedes's house on Saturday morning. It felt like we just needed to plan for one more thing.

When I got home, my mom, who was in the middle of painting the bathroom, asked about the sleepover.

"It was fine."

She pulled a long length of blue tape and lined it up with the trim. Then she handed the tape to me. "Can you do that side?" I knelt on the bathroom tiles. "I knew you would make friends right away," she said.

"Mercedes? Huh," I say. I wouldn't call her a *friend*.

The tape made a belching sound as my mom pulled it off the roll. "You know," she said, "Mercedes is an unusual name."

I shrugged, but my stomach churned as I wondered if my mom actually knew about Mercedes. I thought about Mercedes warning me not to get moms involved.

"Everyone thinks she's named after the car," I said, hoping random conversation might distract my mom.

She laughed. "I imagine they do. But Mercedes is a common Spanish name. In fact, I knew someone named Mercedes a long time ago."

I squinted at her, trying to figure out what she knew. But my mom went back to taping, and I knew then that she doesn't know anything about Mercedes Miller. And I knew that we *had* to go to find Francisco Gómez.

"Get your parents' signatures in by Wednesday," Ms. Garcia is saying, "or you're not going."

"Field trips are the best!" November calls out, pumping his fist.

"Permission slips and appropriate behavior, November Harris."

"Sorry, Ms. Garcia," November says.

November isn't the only one excited about going on a field trip. Around me, kids are shouting about which classes they'll miss and who they'll sit with on the bus. November calls to Ted, "Hey, partners, right?" Ted grins and gives November a thumbs-up.

Who will I sit with? Who will be my partner? I glance around the classroom. I feel very small. Almost invisible. It feels like my first day at Poppy View all over again. Even when I had Mai and Sonja to sit with on the bus, I've always hated field trips. Most people think field trips mean getting out of school for a day, but I like how school is predictable and safe. I don't like not knowing when we'll get a bathroom break or where to get a drink of water. Being somewhere new makes my stomach feel achy.

In first grade, our class went to an apple orchard. It was supposed to be a fun trip with apple picking, a tractor ride, and a hay maze. While we were in the maze, I got separated from my group and the parent chaperone. At first I loved the feeling of being inside the maze surrounded by tall hay bales. I stopped and stared up at the cloudless blue sky. I spotted the faint white disc of the moon. And then my group was gone. I remember panicking, gulping for air. I could hear their voices—their laughter and shouts—but I couldn't see them anywhere. At each corner, I thought I would find someone I knew, see something familiar. But every corner was the same, the same scratchy hay around me and the same sky above me. By the time my teacher found me, I was crying.

"Oooh, look," November says to me in a loud whisper as he passes me a pink permission slip. "Planetarium."

"This presentation will supplement our study of the gravitational pull," Ms. Garcia is saying. She stands with a very straight back at the front of the room. She might be an actual robot—a well-dressed one. "The moon program from the planetarium is spectacular at Northern Madrone. The college has an excellent—"

I snatch the slip of paper. I squint, concentrate.

Parent signature.

School bus.

I need to be sure I'm reading the words carefully.

Northern Madrone College.

I squeeze my eyes shut. My breath is fast and shallow. In my mind, I see the photo of Francisco Gómez standing on the mountainside. I see the paragraph on the screen. *This year's Dupree Visiting Professor at Northern Madrone College.*

It's a sign.

Isn't it? I picture the Operation D.A.D. plan in my notebook. Supplies, bus schedule. I open my eyes. What will Mercedes—

"Ms. Garcia!" I never blurt in class, I always raise my hand. But this is an emergency. She glares at me the same way she glared at November.

"I know you're new, Miss Gómez," Ms. Garcia says in clipped tone, "but we raise our hands here at Poppy View Middle School."

"I, uh, really have to go to the bathroom."

"Hurry back," she snaps.

In the breezeway, I'm still clutching the pink permission slip and my hands are shaking. Is it panic or excitement? All I know is that I've got to find Mercedes. I wish I knew what class she was in now. I walk past my locker and Mrs. Ellingham's classroom. I'm just about to turn around and walk in the other direction when I spot smooth dark-brown hair that's just beginning to frizz. She's sitting in the desk closest to the door. I stop and she looks up. Our eyes meet for half a second and then, before I realize it, she sneaks into the hallway.

"What is it?" she asks. "You don't look so good."

"I'm fine," I say. "I'm good, actually."

She glances over her shoulder. Is she checking to see if the teacher is watching? Or is she worried about the other kids? I know she's embarrassed to be seen with me. She shakes her head. "What's the matter with you?"

"Have you had science class yet?"

She gives me a quizzical look. "No, next class. Why?"

"You'll find out. We're going on a field trip. The whole seventh grade." I hand her the paper. "Look."

Mercedes's face goes pale and then her cheeks burn red. Her brown eyes widen. The amber specks glint in the sunlight.

"It's a sign," we say.

In unison.

CHAPTER 18

Mercedes

T his is what we're going to do," I whisper to Mattie. We're in a handicap stall in the girls bathroom across from Ms. Garcia's room. "We won't say anything, just get on the bus on Friday like everything is normal."

"Can we sit together?" Mattie asks.

I shake my head. Yesterday Gaby and Rebecca group-texted me.

Rebecca: Are you friends with the weird new girl, M?

Mercedes: No. Why would you think that?

Gaby: We saw you with her after school. U didn't notice us.

Mercedes: I told you we had to work on our social studies project. ☹

Luckily, my friends didn't ask any more questions. And I don't want them asking any on Friday.

"You sit with your friends," I tell Mattie firmly, "and I'll sit with mine."

She crosses her arms like she's insulted. I wonder what her life was like before she moved here. She's so weird; she doesn't seem to be able to figure out how to fit in. Like, maybe if she just got a few new T-shirts she wouldn't look so kid-like. We're in seventh grade, after all. She could really use a flat iron, too. Mom bought me one when I was nine.

"It'll be less suspicious," I say. She nods in agreement. Luckily. It's not that I'm embarrassed to be seen with her. I glance at her T-shirt that has a picture of a skunk in a canoe. Okay, it's partly that. "We'll get on the bus, get out with everyone else, and then skip out of the planetarium."

"Ooh!" she cries. I clap a hand over her mouth and shush her.

"Be quiet, Mattie. We don't want Mrs. Leeds coming in here."

She wrenches my hand away. "Well, just now Ms. Garcia let me go, so it'll probably be easy. I didn't think she would. She's so scary. I sometimes think she's—"

"Mattie, we're getting off topic. Can we summarize? We'll sneak out of the field trip and then go find him."

We both jump at a *bang*. Outside of the stall, we hear the bathroom door slam open and then shut. We listen to the click of heels. These are not kid shoes. I peek under the stall. These are teacher shoes.

We stare at each other in frozen silence. I'm afraid the teacher can hear my pounding heart. At last the water runs and the paper towels dispense and the clicking heels click away.

"You'll know where to go, right?" Mattie whispers as soon as the coast is clear. "Since you've been there before?" She has a little hiccup in her voice, like she's trying not to panic.

"It's going to be easy-peasy," I assure her. Although, actually, I have no idea. But she looks so worried, I say, "We'll just get to his office, pop in, and say, 'Hi, we're your kids,' and sneak on the bus back to school. No big deal," I add as if I really believe it's no big deal. "I'm sure we can find one professor in one little college."

Mattie looks at me.

"How hard could it be?"

"I'm still bringing all the stuff for Operation D.A.D."

CHAPTER 19

Mattie

C oming home from school the next day, I almost missed my stop. I was trying to imagine what it will be like to actually meet Francisco Gómez. In four days—no, three and half. I was thinking about the photo on my desk. About my mom and how she had been his actual wife. About how they got divorced before I was born, but if they hadn't, he would be my actual father. Or something. I was thinking about all the things I don't really understand. And then I saw my new house out of the corner of my eye. I had to shout at the bus driver to stop and let me out. I could feel everyone staring at me as I shuffled down the aisle.

When I finally make it through the bright-red front door, I want to collapse on the couch. I want my mom to make me cinnamon toast and pour me a glass of milk and say, "How was your day, Mattie-mouse?"

Instead, even before I take my shoes off, she comes bustling toward me. "When Lucas and Kenny get home, we have to get Kenny to soccer, we need to buy you new shoes, and I need to stop at the library before we make dinner."

"Can I get some nail polish?"

"Nail polish? Oh, Mattie, are you turning into a teenager now?"

"Never mind," I say.

"Well, in any case, can you help me with the laundry first?"

"But—"

"Please, Mattie?"

I follow her to the garage, where, strangely, the washer and dryer are. Not in the basement where laundry rooms belong. Houses in California, my mom told me, don't have basements.

"What happens if there's a tornado? Where does everyone go?" I had asked.

"There aren't tornadoes here, Mattie-mouse," she said brightly.

"Just earthquakes," I said glumly. "Which you can't plan for."

The washer and dryer are pushed against the back wall of the garage. The whole place smells like gasoline and fabric softener and saltwater. There are four overflowing laundry baskets lined up in a row.

"Help me sort the colors." Back home, when it was just the two of us, laundry had been a one-day, two-basket operation. "Let's see. We'll do brights, darks, and whites last." She bends over Lucas's basket and pulls out a plastic brontosaurus. She sighs. "Actually, we'll need more than three loads."

In the drafty garage, I survey the laundry, the boxes of other people's memories in the rafters, Bob's motorcycle under a tarp, Mom's new minivan. What did Bob do before we came along? I think of Francisco Gómez. Does he do his own laundry? Does he have a wife to help him?

When we're done sorting, my mom does actually make me cinnamon toast. Which would have tasted even better if she hadn't also given some to Lucas and Kenny when they got home from school.

After our snack, it's rush, rush, rush. Kenny to soccer, drive across town and get lost finding the shoe store. Cram my feet into new sneakers. Back across town to the library.

"I have to grab a couple things, Mattie," my mom says as we walk in. "Can you keep an eye on Lucas?"

I don't say yes or no.

"I'll make it up to you, I promise," she adds. The look in her eyes makes my stomach feel funny. My mom and I always did everything together. Now there are huge things we don't understand about each other. Like how she's a wife now and a mom to these little boys. And how I'm going to meet my dad on Friday.

"No problem," I say, and head toward the children's room with Lucas.

"Bam!" he shouts, and pretends to shoot a bad guy and then ducks behind a chair. Why can't he be normal—and quiet—for once?

"Put the books you want to take home on this table," I tell him.

"Bam!"

While he rummages through the bins of picture books, I wander around, glancing over every once in a while to make sure Lucas isn't destroying anything. And then a book display on a shelf catches my eye. *Ramona Quimby, Age 8. Ramona the Pest. Beezus and Ramona.* I smile, remembering reading those books when I was about nine or ten. There's a movie, too. I love how Beezus is the cool older sister and Ramona is a pest. Those books made me wish I wasn't an only child. I peer around the bookshelf and see Lucas the Pest amazingly piling books on the table as instructed. I guess I'm not an only child now. I have two stepbrothers. And a sister. Well, half sister. Who would be Beezus and who would be Ramona?

Just as I'm wondering this, I hear a small voice say, "One more."

There, in a cozy reading nook under a poster of an alien jumping out of a book, I spot her. Mercedes is with a little boy about Lucas's age. The boy has blond hair and long eyelashes. He's curled up in Mercedes's lap. She leans forward, reading aloud to him. Her face is calm, quiet, with half a smile on her lips. This is nothing like the loud, show-off, popular Mercedes I've seen at school. Nothing like the cool and aloof Mercedes she is with me. This is a completely different Mercedes. Somehow, I know she wouldn't want me to see her like this.

I silently reach out and grab Lucas's pile of books, add *Beezus and Ramona* to the stack, and motion for him to follow me. Luckily, Lucas does the most un-Lucas-like thing: he quietly follows me to the checkout desk.

CHAPTER 20

Mercedes

Y our mom just called," Cristina says when she picks up
      Tristan and me from the library.
      "Why didn't she call me?" I ask. I pull my phone
out of my pocket. Dead.

When we get home, I go into Mom's office. It has a glass
desk facing the ocean, and her orchids, ferns, and other growing stuff frame the windows. She says she loves her plants, but
Cristina is the one who has to water and feed them. Mom left a
schedule printed out on the windowsill. Cristina doesn't know
much about plants, but she manages to keep them alive.

I plug in my phone to one of Mom's million chargers and
twist and turn in her silver wheelie office chair. The phone
chirps to life and I call Mom. She answers on the first ring and
her face pops into my screen.

"Konnichiwa!" she says. Her favorite Japanese word. "Hi,
sweetie."

"Hi, Mom."

"Are you in my office?" she asks. I nod. "Show me my
babies! Is Cristina taking care of them?"

I pan the camera across the plants.

Mom brings her face close to the camera. "Oh, look how beautiful they are. The phalaenopsis is blooming!"

"Mom," I say, "I don't need to see your pores. Back up a bit."

She holds the phone at a normal distance. I can see that she's in a hotel dining room. It's morning there, already tomorrow. If I were in Japan, I would be one day closer to meeting Frank Gómez.

"How's Tristan? Did he get the samurai sword I sent?"

I can't help but roll my eyes. This is the second sword she's sent him since she's been in Tokyo. "Yes, Mom."

"And did you get the anime books? Aren't they great?"

When I was in fifth grade, I was really into watching anime, then I got into manga. Now that I'm almost a teenager, I would be more excited if she sent me some Japanese lotion with green tea or whatever. I nod anyway. "When are you coming home?" I ask like I always do.

"You know the answer, Mercedes."

I do know the answer. I just keep hoping that one of these times, when I ask, her answer will be "tomorrow." I would even settle for "next week." It never is.

"Thanksgiving. I know."

You would think that the owner of a successful company could just stay home with her kids and let other people do all the work. But she says she needs to be there in person. Ever since Tristan started kindergarten last year, she's been gone for longer and longer trips. I think of my own trip. I told Mattie I wasn't nervous, but when I really try to imagine meeting our dad, I feel all mixed up.

"Hey, Mom, I was wondering—" I begin to say. This is it. I'm going to ask her about Mattie. I'm going to ask her about Frank. I'm going to ask her all the things I've asked before and maybe this time will be different.

"This project is going really well," she says. She hasn't heard me. She didn't even realize I was speaking. This time isn't different. She's not looking at the camera anymore but at some point in the distance. "But I have to manage every step. In fact, I'm sorry, sweetie, but I've got to go put out a fire right now."

I had to explain to Tristan what she means when she says "put out a fire." She doesn't mean the hotel is on fire. It means somebody needs her for something. Tristan had looked at me and said, "Sometimes I wish we were the fire."

"Okay, Mom," I say. "Talk to you soon." Her face disappears from the screen. I guess I won't find out anything today.

Friday can't get here soon enough.

CHAPTER 21

Mattie

Before I know it, it's Friday—way too soon. I pull the blinds open in my room. No fog today, just a slow California sunrise. I stare at the clothes in my closet. I know they aren't quite right. What do you wear to go meet your father? I pull on my comfy jeans and my new T-shirt. It says *Santa Cruz* and has a picture of a skateboard. Even though it's new, I can tell it's not quite what other kids at Poppy View Middle School wear. But I still haven't figured out exactly what that is. Maybe I need to paint my fingernails? Sometimes the smallest details can make the biggest difference.

Then I take everything out of my backpack. Time to double-check Operation D.A.D. I load my backpack with all my supplies—well, not the change of clothes or the rain jacket. It doesn't look like rain and it's not like we're staying overnight.

Without those things, my backpack still seems very empty for such a momentous day. What else do I need? What do you take with you when you're going to meet your father for the first time? I look around my room. What would show him who I am, what I'm like? If we only have a few minutes with him before we sneak back to the bus, it'll have to be just the right thing.

My self-portrait from last year's art class is on my bulletin board above my desk. I'm really proud of the eyes. Then I study it closer and realize the eyes look more like Mercedes's than mine. I unpin the portrait and stuff it in a desk drawer. I have another drawing of our old house in Minnesota. Should I bring that? Then I realize that he knows that house; that's the house they lived in when they were married. I shove that in the desk drawer, too, and then look around my room again.

My favorite book is on my nightstand. *The Little Prince*. It's an old, worn copy that was my mom's when she was a kid. My mom used to read it aloud to me when I was little. Even though I never read it anymore, I just like having it nearby. The book is about a little boy who comes to Earth from outer space. That's how I felt on my first day at Poppy View—like I had just arrived on a new planet. My favorite page is the picture of the Little Prince on his planet, Asteroid B-612, which isn't much bigger than a car. All around him in the drawing are stars and planets swirling around his asteroid. He looks like he's the center of the universe but also like everyone has forgotten about him. That's how I feel sometimes.

But I don't want to carry a book around on the field trip. I bet Mercedes would make fun of me. I leave *The Little Prince* where it is and head to the kitchen.

It's total chaos in here, as usual. Kenny is watching You-Tube videos at full volume on his dad's tablet. Bob is reading bits of news stories to my mom. Lucas is running in circles around the kitchen island, singing a song I recognize from his favorite cartoon show about a rat and mouse that solve mysteries. No one notices me.

I take my lunch bag and water bottle from the fridge and stuff it in my backpack. Mom turns around then and sees me. She calls over the noise, "What do you want for breakfast?"

My stomach grumbles, but I say, "I'm not hungry."

Is it a lie, I wonder, if you don't say something true? The truth is that today is the day I'm going to meet my dad and I'm too nervous to eat. But I can't tell my mom. My mom looks so worn out. Happy but worn out. And I don't want to worry her. It also feels like this truth is my truth, my secret. Is a secret the same as a lie?

"Well, take a granola bar with you." She tosses me one with an expert throw. I fumble the catch and when it drops on the floor, Kenny laughs. I can't tell if he's laughing at me or at his screen. Lucas yells something about dinosaurs and spills his milk. "Have fun at your field trip," Mom calls after me as I slip out the front door.

Getting one hundred and twenty seventh graders on three yellow school buses is more chaos than even the kitchen at the Jasper house. Teachers call out, kids shove and push, buses belch black smoke. Mrs. Leeds emerges from her office to try to maintain order. "Make sure you have your lunches!" she calls out. "But no cell phones! Leave the cell phones in your lockers!"

"You heard Mrs. Leeds," Ms. Garcia repeats, her voice stern. She's wearing black boots, a yellow sweater, and a green jacket. Long yellow-and-green earrings dangle from her ears. "If you brought a phone, march back to your locker right now. Detention for anyone caught with a phone on the field trip."

Most of us stumble back to the seventh-grade wing. The clank of lockers opening and closing adds to the confusion. I don't see Mercedes anywhere. I set my phone on top of my language arts book. I hope we don't need our phones for our secret mission today. I slam my locker door. *It'll be fine,* I tell myself.

When the seventh grade is finally on the buses, I sit with Sunny. November and Ted are in the seat ahead of us.

"Are you afraid of the dark?" November pops up to ask me.

"No," I say. I'm afraid of a lot of things, but not the dark. "Why?"

"Well, it's dark in a planetarium. Have you been to one before? In fourth grade, we went to one in San Francisco."

"Of course," I tell November. "We do have things like planetariums in Minnesota."

Now Ted's head pops up. "Minnesota. Capital is Saint Paul."

"That's where I used to live," I remind him.

Ted and November talk about capital cities and then argue about which one they'd like to live in. The only city I want to live in is the one I came from. I miss the stately two-story houses and the leafy green ash trees in Saint Paul. Outside the bus's windows, I watch pink flowering bushes and the occasional palm tree whip past small stucco houses and advertisements for wetsuits. Soon the bus rumbles onto the highway. Bringing us closer to Northern Madrone College. And Francisco Gómez.

"Have you been to Northern Madrone before?" I ask Sunny. Even though she's so quiet, I'm grateful to have someone to sit with.

"I think so?" She's so shy, it makes me nervous.

I lean over the seat. "Hey, guys, have you ever been to this college?"

November and Ted pop up again. "We saw a concert there last year, didn't we?" November says to Sunny. "It was dope, wasn't it?" A look of recognition flashes across her face and she nods. "Violins and cellos," November says.

The corners of Sunny's serious mouth turn up just a bit. "Screech, screech, screech," she imitates in her squeaky voice.

We all laugh. I guess she's kind of funny.

I pull out the map of the campus that Mercedes printed for Operation D.A.D. "Do you know your way around the college?"

Ted grabs the map. "Sure. Here's the building where we saw the boring concert. Mrs. Leeds started snoring—do you remember?" Ted laughs and then snorts. I hear a soft chirp beside me—the sound of Sunny laughing the quietest laugh. "Look, Mattie," he says. "This is where we're going. Science and Engineering Building."

"What's this oval?" Sunny squeaks.

"That's the swimming pool."

"I wish we were going swimming!" November shouts.

"How about this?" I point to a square of green.

"That's the Quad," Ted says. I'm impressed he knows all this stuff.

"His mom is a professor at UC Santa Cruz," November informs us.

That must explain why he has Wikipedia in his head instead of a brain like the rest of us.

"Go, Banana Slugs," Ted says, and snorts again. I have no idea what he's talking about.

"That's the mascot for UC Santa Cruz," November explains.

"What's the Quad for?" I ask, trying to get his attention back to the map of Northern Madrone College. I need to figure out where we're going. We won't have very much time once we arrive.

"The Quad is where the students hang out when they're not in class. Look, here's the library."

"Have you been to other buildings?" I ask as casually as I can. We figured out that Francisco Gómez's office is in the anthropology department, which is in the Humanities Building.

But instead of answering, Ted says, "And this is the track. November, remember when we did that soccer clinic? I think it was there."

I sigh; it's hopeless. It's impossible to keep those two on topic.

When the boys start bopping me and Sunny with long whips of licorice from Ted's lunch, I snatch the map out of his hands and shove it in my backpack. Ms. Garcia catches them, and she sits in their seat with them. Now I can't ask any more questions. Beside me, Sunny is silent. And I'm glad. I lean my head against the window and watch the cars and trees whiz past. I can hear Ms. Garcia telling November about the moon program we're going to see. He's telling her about a meteor shower he saw with his dad. The bus barrels north along the ocean. I don't care about moons or planetariums, meteors, or licorice. I'm going to meet my father today.

CHAPTER 22

Mercedes

Every time the bus takes a curve, Gaby and Rebecca lean into me, giggling, throwing me off balance, squishing me into the window.

"Whoa!" they shriek. "Watch out, Mercedes!"

I laugh the first couple times, but now I just want some quiet. I need time to think before we arrive at Northern Madrone College.

"Here we go!" Gaby yells on the next curve.

"Cut it out!" I snap at her, and push against her with all my strength. And when I get mad, I have a lot of strength. Rebecca, who's on the aisle, tips right out. She lands with a thud on the dirty floor of the bus.

"You're so rude, Mercedes," Rebecca yells. "Look at my pants."

Even though we were supposed to leave our phones in our lockers, Gaby pulls out hers. She snaps a picture.

"Gaby!" Rebecca shrieks. "You're going to get us in trouble!"

Mrs. Ellingham strides down the aisle toward us, leaning on the backs of the seats for balance. "That's enough, girls. Gaby, hand me the phone. You know better than that. Get up, Rebecca. I'm going to separate you three."

And that's how I end up sitting next to Ruben Hernandez, who is the second quietest kid in seventh grade after Sunny Li. When he actually talks out loud, he speaks English with a rickety accent because he's from Mexico and hasn't been in Santa Cruz for very long. On every curve, he braces himself so he won't bump into me. Good.

I watch the ocean go by out the window, feeling us getting closer and closer to Northern Madrone College and Frank Gómez. What will he be like? Will he be loud and confident like me? Or will he be nervous and serious like Mattie? Will he know which of us is which? I picture us walking into his office and saying, *Hi, we're your daughters. Matilde and Mercedes. Nice to meet you.* And he'll be so happy to see us, he'll leap out of his chair and hug us both so tight we won't be able to breathe. *You're here at last!* he'll say. Wait—I suppose he'll have a Spanish accent. I rewind my imagining and replay it with Frank sounding a little bit like Ruben. The only Spanish words I know are from watching *Dora the Explorer*. I glance at Ruben. Maybe I should ask him how to say, "We're your daughters" in Spanish.

At last, we're at Northern Madrone College. My fingers tingle like they do before a race. The buses come to a stop in the guest parking lot. At one end is the athletic building that I recognize from the cross-country meet. Behind it, there's a peek of the sparkling blue water of the swimming pool. Eucalyptus trees dot the campus and make the whole college feel dark and secret, but in a cool way. As everyone jostles to get off the bus, I pull the campus map out of my back pocket. Beyond the athletic building is the student union, to the right is the arts building, and past that is the science building where the planetarium is. I can't see it, but I know from the map that at the other end of the parking lot is the Humanities Building. Easy-peasy.

"Can you believe Mrs. Ellingham?" Gaby says. "That was so unfair that she split us up. I had to sit with Charlotte Perkins." Gaby keeps complaining, but I stop listening to her. I'm trying to figure out how I'm going to escape her and Rebecca. At school, I love having people around me all the time. I love when we hang out at my locker before class starts and just talk. I never really listen to them, but I like having the noise around me, the attention. I don't know how Mattie can stand it. I've seen her at her locker by herself in the mornings. I hate being alone. It's so, well, lonely. But today I need to lose my friends.

"Gaby Molina," calls Mrs. Ellingham, "move along. You're blocking the aisle."

Gaby smirks and then heads to the door, giving me a great idea.

As the seventh graders march toward the science building, I catch a glimpse of Mattie. She's walking by herself, although the dork crew is close behind her. She's pale. I hope she's okay. I shake the thought away. It's not my fault if she's having a panic attack or whatever. She agreed to do this. I didn't force her. I mean, not exactly.

We file into the planetarium, which has weird seats that lean way back. The whole room is lit with pale-blue lights, making it feel like you should rub your eyes so you can see better. Everything is carpeted—the floors, the aisle, even the walls. The carpet soaks up all the shrieks and hollers of the noisy kids. Gaby and Rebecca are on my heels as we head down the right-hand aisle. When I pause, Rebecca bumps into me. Time to put my plan into action.

"Watch out, Becca," I say, and shove her back. She laughs and pushes me. I glance up to see where Ms. Garcia is.

"It wasn't me," Rebecca says, playfully elbowing Gaby. I laugh too loudly and my friends imitate me. It's like I've been training for this my whole life. No one will guess that I'm *trying* to get us in trouble. We keep laughing and shoving. And then Ms. Garcia's eyes are on us. Just like I planned.

"Girls, I've already separated you once before. Clearly you cannot handle sitting together. You, Gaby, sit there. Rebecca, you take the seat up front." Ms. Garcia is pointing left, then right. She looks at me. "Mercedes, you park yourself right here." She points to a seat in the second row from the back, only a few feet from the door we entered.

Perfectly positioned for sneaking out.

As the lights dim, I spot Mattie again. She's sitting at the other end of the half circle of seats. Near the other exit door. Her eyes are huge. She glances across at me. We catch each other's eyes for the split second before we're plunged into darkness.

"Woooo!" call out the boys as we sit in the planetarium, our eyes trying to adjust to the dark. Someone shouts a curse word and then I hear Ms. Garcia. "Adam, Dante, and Joaquin, do you three want detention?"

I keep squinting in the blackness, and pretty soon pinpricks of light pop up above me. One by one, the glow of stars appears like very dim and very slow-motion fireworks. Humming music thrums through speakers, louder and louder, until it feels like we're floating in an upside-down bowl of glitter.

Once, when Tristan was a baby, Tristan's dad took us camping. We drove into the mountains and set up a green tent in a clearing. I remember roasting marshmallows and feeling bad that Tristan was too little to eat them. When it was time to go to bed, his dad put out the fire with a bucket of water, sending clouds of smoke into the sky. Once the smoke cleared, we were in total darkness. Tristan was asleep in his car seat, but Mom and I leaned back on the picnic table and looked up at the sky. We just sat there for a few minutes, in silence, staring at the night sky. And then Tristan's dad pointed out which constellations were which. Mom kept correcting him (she knows the constellations because she grew up on a farm). He got offended, and then she got mad at him. Tristan started to cry, and his dad ended up sleeping in the car.

"Today," says a gentle, melodic voice over a speaker, "we're going to visit the moon and take a quick trip to the edges of our solar system." The woman's soothing, sleepy voice tells everyone to turn off their cell phones—even though we weren't supposed to have them. I pat my sweatshirt pocket to make sure mine is still hidden there. "Where we're going, our phones won't work anyway." Then she tells us more rules like not talking or kicking the seat in front of us.

"Some people get dizzy during our adventure. If that happens to you, just close your eyes. You should feel better soon. If not, follow the aisles marked with red lights to exit the auditorium."

It's too dark to find Mattie, but I hope she realizes that we have a perfect excuse now for sneaking out. As I'm thinking about what's coming next, the stars above start moving. Or are we moving? As they turn, the edge of the ceiling gets brighter. I can make out the silhouette of trees and a couple houses. Then an orange glow.

"Sunrise," the voice says. The orange glow fades again. "Then sunset. As the earth spins on its axis, the glow of the sun sinks over the horizon, giving way to other celestial sights. First we see the brightest star, the planet Jupiter, slip above the tree line."

Little by little, more stars appear.

"There's Venus. Saturn. Mercury. The planets."

Each time she names one, it twinkles brighter for a moment so we can see which one she's talking about. I remember seeing the star winking at me from my bedroom window. I get that sticky feeling again. Then the music changes rhythm. "We'll be traveling at the speed of light to take a detour to the outer edges of our solar system." Suddenly the pinpricks of stars morph into streaks of bright light. The room spins and twirls. The music pulses in my ears, knocking, trying to enter my brain. The lights glow brighter and brighter. The lines spin. I squeeze my eyes shut. The woman said I would feel better if I closed my eyes. Well, she was wrong. The music is swelling and swirling, making me feel like I'm the only person in the universe. An awful feeling of loneliness claws at my throat. I open one eye. My stomach bounces. I shut it again. Now I'm even more dizzy. I open my eyes. Lights flash. Close my eyes. Open. I peek at the floor and find the red glow of the aisle.

I have to get out of here.

CHAPTER 23

Mattie

When I see Mercedes sneak out the rear door of the planetarium, I know it's now or never. To break the rules. To go someplace new. To find my father. I clutch my backpack, then stop. But—what would happen if I don't follow? I picture Mercedes, with her confident voice and easy smile, meeting Francisco Gómez, maybe telling him his other daughter didn't want to meet him. I imagine them strolling into the sunset on one of Santa Cruz's beaches. I shake my head. That's not the way it's supposed to happen. I can feel it deep inside. I can't explain the feeling. The certainty that this is what has to happen right now. I need to meet my father.

I stumble out of my seat, dragging my Operation D.A.D. supplies behind me. Luckily, everyone seems mesmerized by a sudden splash of starlight that streaks across the auditorium and no one notices me making my escape.

When I emerge, I'm blinded by the lights in the hallway. At first I don't see Mercedes. Where is she? What if she left already? Is she walking into the sunset with our father? Then I spot her. She's on the floor, her head between her knees.

"What's the matter?"

She shakes her head but doesn't look up.

"Are you okay?" I crouch next to her. She doesn't answer. "Did you get in trouble?" I glance up and down the hallway. At our end is the door from the auditorium and in the other direction is a glass doorway leading outside. No teachers in sight. It's just us.

"What is it?" I ask.

"I'm fine," she snaps, but she doesn't move.

"Did you get dizzy? Do you need to lie down?"

She doesn't answer but she slumps farther down the wall until she's lying on the floor.

"Here, have some water." I pull my water bottle out of my backpack.

Mercedes lifts her head. Her face is sort of pale. But her eyes are angry. She snatches the water bottle from me and gulps.

I sit next to her. What will I do if she's sick? I can't go find Francisco Gómez by myself.

"Are you—"

"I'm fine," she says again. She doesn't look at me as she moves back to sitting. Then she slowly stands, batting away my hand when I try to help her. She's a little unsteady, but then she seems to regain her balance. Her color is returning. "Here." She shoves my bottle in my face.

"Aren't you glad for Operation D.A.D.?" I ask. "It's good to be prepared."

She shoots daggers from her brown eyes. "Let's go," Mercedes commands. "That direction." She says this in a bossy way, even though we only have two options: back where we came from or keep going. I follow her out the glass door to the campus of Northern Madrone College.

. . .

"I don't think you're supposed to go that way," I call to Mercedes. Instead of taking the sidewalk that hugs the science building, she's crossed a grassy lawn toward a fence and some trees.

"It's a shortcut."

I run after her. Mercedes stays a few feet in front of me. I keep looking over my shoulder, checking to see if Ms. Garcia or Mrs. Ellingham saw us. But there is no one. No one to see two seventh graders wander away from a field trip at Northern Madrone College.

When I reach her, she's at the fence that divides the path from the black oval track I saw on the map. "I've been on that track," Mercedes says, watching a woman running. She's alone, her arms pumping back and forth, her legs in rhythm. I don't understand people who run without a reason. "There was a cross-country meet here last summer."

"I hate running. I almost died last week when we had to run the mile run."

Mercedes looks at me like I just admitted to hating ice cream. "Running is the best. You just go. It's you and the ground. Doesn't matter what anyone else does. You're in a race with yourself."

I study the runner on the track. She does look like she doesn't hate it. "Are you really the fastest—" I stop when I see that she's holding her phone. "Your phone? Mrs. Leeds made us put our phones in our lockers at school!" I cry. "How did you get to keep yours?"

"What? You never broke a rule before?" She keeps tapping.

"It's a good thing I kept it. What if there's an emergency? You'll be glad I broke the rules. Besides, I'm texting Rebecca—luckily she didn't get hers confiscated. I'm telling her to cover for me."

Oh.

Mercedes puts her phone in her back pocket and turns toward the path. "What are you waiting for?"

We leave the solo runner and follow the sidewalk around a bend and another bunch of trees. In front of us are two buildings. The one directly in front of us says SMILEY ARTS BUILDING in yellow metal letters. To our right is a smaller building. I can't see the sign, but Mercedes heads in that direction.

"Humanities Building," she breathes. "Home of the anthropology department."

We approach the big double doors, and then, as if we choreographed it, we both come to a halt. If we were cartoon characters, there would have been skid marks and a plume of dust, we stopped so fast. We just stand there, side by side, staring at the entrance of the Humanities Building at Northern Madrone College, with the knowledge that, sitting at a desk, in an office, in this building, will be our father. Francisco Gómez.

"Can I help you?"

A young woman in overalls and a long sweater carries two paper cups of coffee. Her sunglasses are pushed on her head.

"No, sorry, we just—" Mercedes says. "We're just waiting for someone."

I nod vigorously.

"Who? Can I help?" the young woman asks.

"Our mom," we say in an unplanned but coordinated lie.

"Our mom is just finishing some work," Mercedes lies. She

does it so well, I have to admire her. "We're supposed to meet her at"—she checks her smartwatch—"eleven. She'll be here soon."

"You can wait inside if you want," the woman says. "There's a lounge on the first floor." She hits the automatic-door-opener button with her hip and walks through with her coffees.

We look at each other.

"Um, thanks," Mercedes says.

The lounge is two sofas and two chairs to the left of the entrance. I sit cautiously on one of the hard seats, catching my breath. What are we doing? I check the clock on the wall behind me. We've only been gone from the planetarium for fifteen minutes, but it feels like hours. Like a lifetime.

Mercedes doesn't sit with me. She wanders around the foyer of the Humanities Building reading flyers and looking at the art on the walls. It must remind her of home and her mom.

I can't believe we just lied to that woman. My actual mom doesn't know that I sneaked away from a field trip, and she would never guess I would do such a thing. My heart rate speeds up and my breath gets ragged. What if the woman comes back and asks who our mom is? My arms are tingly. What if we can't find the office? I'm definitely having a heart attack. What if Francisco Gómez doesn't want to meet us? My feet feel like they've disappeared. What if he hates us? What if he calls our moms and we get in huge trouble? What if he calls the police? What if—

"Mattie, stop spiraling." Mercedes's voice is sharp.

Did I say all that out loud?

"I wasn't—"

"Yes, you were."

How did she know?

"You can stop destroying your T-shirt. It didn't do anything to you, you know."

I look down at the surfboard. I didn't even realize that I was picking at a loose thread and now the entire hem of my new shirt is unraveling. Just like me.

It's just a panic episode, I hear my mom whisper in my mind. I take a deep, deep breath. Then I get up and stand next to Mercedes. She's looking at a big sign on the brick wall that says DIRECTORY.

"Anthropology department is down this hall." She points.

I push all thoughts of panic aside. No spiraling, especially not in front of Mercedes. I follow her down the hall, even though I'm pretty sure I'm not ready for whatever comes next.

CHAPTER 24

Mercedes

I try to ignore the irritating squeak of Mattie's sneakers behind me. This is it. We're going to meet him. My dad. *Our* dad. Frank Gómez.

Once, I asked Mom why he didn't send Christmas cards like everyone else we knew. There was always a pile of cards in the basket by the front door. From great-uncles, second cousins, Mom's high school classmates and old boyfriends. There were long holiday letters from her former assistant and my old babysitters. The people we knew best didn't send cards. They called us or came over on Christmas Day for a big dinner, the one time a year we used our long dining room table. But Frank Gómez didn't come over and he never sent a card.

"I suppose he doesn't have our address," Mom had told me.

"What?" I asked. "He doesn't know where I live?"

"No," Mom said. "Why would he need to?"

"Is that why he never visits? Because he doesn't know where to find me?" What I was thinking but didn't say was, *Please tell me it isn't that he doesn't want to.*

But Mom just sighed. "He wouldn't visit even if he had your address, Mercedes. He's far away and very busy." She tucked a strand of hair behind my ear. "You don't need him."

But I wasn't sure. Tristan had his dad. Where was mine? Why didn't my dad want to visit?

"But he knows about me, right?"

She nodded. "Of course. I told him about you, sent him your picture. You were such a cute baby."

"What about the other baby? His other daughter?" I had asked Mom. I hated the words "other daughter." It made me feel like a designer knockoff, like the fake Gucci bags they sell by the Boardwalk. A cheap imitation.

"Well, the other daughter is probably not a baby anymore," Mom said. She laughed and I felt the anger boiling.

"Does *she* have my address?"

Mom shook her head. "I've told you: Frank Gómez's other daughter lives far away. I doubt we'll ever meet her or her mother. *He* probably hasn't even met her. You don't need random strangers, Mercedes. We have each other. And you have your brother." Then Mom stood up like she did when she was done with a conversation.

As we get closer to the anthropology department, I get a strange feeling in my toes. What if Mom was right? What if he doesn't want to meet me? What if he only wants to meet Mattie? His first daughter? I shake my head. Is this what it feels like to be Mattie? To worry about everything?

"Can I help you?"

I stop and Mattie bumps into me. Blocking our way is a woman in a green fleece jacket over a blue dress. She's wearing striped tights and brown clogs. Hopeless fashion sense. The door from which the woman has appeared says: ANTHROPOLOGY DEPARTMENT. PLEASE KNOCK IF DOOR IS LOCKED.

"Um, hi," I say. "Just looking for—" My voice cracks. I cough, clear my throat.

"Our brother," Mattie says.

The woman taps her clogged foot. "Who? Do you two know where you're going?" Her arms are full of papers. "I have to go. I'm late."

She doesn't wait for us to answer before she clogs away, a disastrous style blur around the corner.

"Now what?"

I shrug and continue into the maze of corridors. I can feel the nervous ball of energy behind me that is Mattie. The doors along the hallway are closed. Each one has a little plaque on it with a room number and a name. The office doors have flyers taped to them. And postcards. And sticky notes. Some have printed schedules, some have cartoons cut from magazines.

This is completely different from Mom's office. She works in a tall glass building in San Francisco. The wall of windows in her office faces the Bay Bridge. The room is so big, it has a couch and an espresso maker and a whole conference table. Her assistant always has a bowl of M&Ms that has a little silver spoon so that you don't touch the candies when you take some. The other people at Mom's work are in smaller offices, but there are so many windows both into the rooms and looking out at the city. The furniture and the carpet and walls are sleek white and bright green to match her company's logo.

This hallway of offices at Northern Madrone College is nothing like a downtown office. It's totally depressing. There are no windows, and the only light comes from flickering bulbs over our heads. Outside some of the offices' closed doors are chairs for people to wait. None of the chairs match—some are wooden with orange seats, some are blue plastic, and one isn't a chair at all, just a stool with three legs.

And then, we see it.

ROOM H-122

DUPREE VISITING PROFESSOR

PROF. F. GOMEZ FLORES

All the blood in my entire body seems to rush first to my hands and then back to my brain. This is it. We are really going to meet him. What will he say? What will I say? What will Mattie say?

"Wow," Mattie says, barely a whisper.

"Yeah," I whisper back.

We stare at the door to our father's office. There are no sticky notes, but there are two postcards taped next to the plaque with his name.

"Look," she says, pointing to the postcard of a green mountain beside a turquoise blue sea.

"Looks like Mexico. Mom took us on vacation in Cancún." I flip the edge of the postcard over. It says *Santa Marta* in swirly letters. "This must be in Colombia."

"I've never been out of the country," Mattie says, awe in her voice.

I stare at her. "For real? But your mom was married to Frank Gómez. I would think she'd love to travel or whatever."

Mattie shakes her head. "Too expensive, I guess. When I grow up, I'm going to travel around the world." The other postcard is a picture of two people dressed in feathers and skirt-type things. It looks like it's from one of those old *National Geographic* magazines that the school librarian is always trying to get us to look at. "I want to see people like this in person." Mattie reaches out and touches the face of the woman in the picture.

"Can I help you?"

This time the adult standing behind us is a guy with dread-locks and a gray plaid sports coat.

"Um," I say. Why can't I seem to get any words out?

"Are you looking for Professor Gómez?" We watch the young man slide a piece of paper under the closed office door. He stands up and looks at us. "Are you two related to him?"

I don't even have to look at Mattie to know she's turning as red as I am.

"We're just visiting because, um, our uncle is, um, waiting for us in the car in the, um . . ." I look at Mattie. "In the parking lot. And we have to just check something—"

The man looks at his phone and then back at us. He's not listening to me. "I think he was headed to the library."

CHAPTER 25

Mattie

According to the campus map, the library is past the science building, across a field, through the Quad. "Come on," I say, and pull her into the sunshine. "This way."

We retrace our steps. The track is empty now. We slip through the trees and round the corner of the science building toward the Quad.

"There you are." It's Mrs. Ellingham. I just about jump out of my skin.

My heart is pounding so hard, I'm sure my teacher can hear it. I can't move, I can't speak. This is it. Two weeks into my new year at a new school, and I'm already going to be the biggest troublemaker in the seventh grade. My mom is going to be so disappointed and Kenny will laugh at me and the welcoming committee won't welcome me at lunch anymore.

"You must have found the other bathrooms." Mrs. Ellingham smiles. "The line did get pretty long."

"Yeah," Mercedes says, a faltering smile on her face. "The line was so much shorter. Thanks for the tip, Mrs. Ellingham."

I just stare at Mercedes. She's quick.

"Is that okay if we head back to our groups now?"

In front of us, in the grassy lawn next to the planetarium doors, kids from our school sit in small groups eating their lunches. I spot November, Ted, and Sunny. Ms. Garcia is patrolling the fence along the pools. My heart slowly returns to its normal rhythm.

"Yes, run along." Mrs. Ellingham is already turning away from us, heading toward Ms. Garcia.

"I can't believe it!" I hiss. "We almost got caught!"

Mercedes stops walking. "That was nothing," she says. "Now, you go your way and I'll go mine. Act normal. Meet you . . ." Mercedes looks around. She points to a little grove of trees next to the science building. "Meet you over there when lunch is over. Make sure Ms. Garcia sees you and counts you before you escape."

"Escape? Again?"

Mercedes looks around to see if anyone is watching us. No one is, not even the teachers. She grabs me by the shoulders. "Mattie. We're staying here until we find him. Get your friends to cover for you. We've got to find the library. We're not going back with the field trip."

"We're not?" I feel itchy.

"No, if we have to, we can take the city bus back."

"But. The plan?"

"Exactly. That's why we studied the transit schedule."

"I thought—"

"Or I can get Cristina to drive us home. Focus, Mattie. All you need to do is get someone to cover for you and meet me over there. And make sure Ms. Garcia counts you!"

And then she's gone.

"But—?"

None of this was part of the Operation D.A.D. plan written in my notebook. Now what? How am I supposed to get away? What if I can't? What if my new friends won't cover for me? Then I won't find my father. I clench my teeth, willing myself not to cry.

"Mattie!" November is calling and waving. "Over here."

I paste a fake smile on my face, just like Mercedes did, and wave at November and Ted and Sunny.

"Where did you go?" November asks with his mouth full.

"Me?"

Sunny mumbles something.

"What?"

"You snuck out," she repeats. The corners of her mouth curl in a grin.

November and Ted have stopped chewing and they're now looking at me like I'm today's entertainment.

"You noticed?" They nod. "Did the teachers notice?"

Sunny shakes her head.

I measure the distance between here and the grove of trees. How will I get there? I'm going to need some help. "Can you guys keep a secret?"

They nod solemnly.

"Okay." Here goes nothing. "My dad works here," I say. This part is not technically a lie. "And I need to go meet him. So, I'm wondering if you can help me, um, sneak out."

"Why doesn't he just come pick you up? I'm sure it would be fine," Ted says. "Since it's your dad."

"He, um, has a class and can't get out in time." *This* is a lie. "I'm supposed to meet him"—another lie— "and get a ride home with him, too." More lies.

"Why don't you just have your mom call Ms. Garcia?" Ted asks. He is too logical.

"Well, my parents are divorced." This is not a lie.

"Oh, I get it. So are mine," November says.

"You see, my dad forgot to write a note for the teachers. And I don't want to get him in trouble with, um, my mom."

"I hate when my parents get mad at each other over custody stuff."

I nod like I know what he means, although my parents don't fight and there is no custody stuff. Just my mom.

"We got your back, Mattie," November assures me. "Don't we?"

Ted shrugs and nods.

Sunny mumbles something.

"What?"

"Just make sure Ms. Garcia counts you after lunch. That'll help." Sunny may be the shyest girl I've ever met, but she's also one of the nicest.

"Got it," I say. I'm so relieved, I want to hug each of them. I feel my pulse slowing. Okay, I have a plan again. Get counted. Meet Mercedes.

"Poppy View seventh graders!" It's Ms. Garcia shouting. "Seventh graders! Throw out your trash and line up!"

I haven't even had time to take one bite of sandwich, but I join the line of kids dumping garbage into two cans next to the double doors to the science building. The grove is a couple dozen feet to the right. I have an idea. My hands are shaking by the time I get to Ms. Garcia. I drop my uneaten sandwich in the trash can. I feel Ms. Garcia tap me lightly on the shoulder and mutter, "Gómez. Fifty-two."

That's when I let the balled-up paper napkin in my hand go. The breeze grabs it and the napkin tumbles away. "Oops!" I say loudly, and step out of line, chasing the trash as it tumbles to the right. Ms. Garcia doesn't look up.

CHAPTER 26

Mercedes

You're back!" Gaby shouts. "Rebecca got your text! Where'd you go?"

I flop on the grass. "Not so loud," I say. "The whole point of sneaking out is to not get caught."

"No one even noticed you were gone," Rebecca says.

"Thanks, Becca." I sit up, opening my lunch bag and taking out my sushi tray. "I'm starving."

I shove California rolls in my mouth while Gaby and Rebecca tell me about the planetarium show and how Adam Collins got in trouble for making fart noises or something. I laugh along with them, but I'm not really paying attention. I need to figure out how to sneak over to our meeting spot without getting caught by Ms. Garcia *and* without my friends seeing that I'm with Mattie Gómez. And I need a good story to tell Gaby and Rebecca.

"Mercedes, can you go to the mall with us tomorrow?" Gaby asks.

"Yeah," says Rebecca, "you have to go because I have to get a new swimming suit. I need your opinion. Please?"

Normally, I would love to hang out at the mall with my best friends. Normally, I wouldn't pass up the opportunity to give advice and share my opinion. Normally, I wouldn't think about it, just say yes. But this is not normal. "I'll have to check with Cristina," I say. I have an idea. "But right now, I need one more favor."

"Ooh, what now?" Rebecca leans forward.

"You have to help me sneak out again."

"Why?" Gaby asks. I shoot her a look and she says, "I mean, okay, what can we do?"

I make up a whole story about how Cristina is taking me shopping in San Francisco today. I tell them that Cristina wants to pick me up from here since it's closer to the city, that she forgot to check with the school, that I don't want her to get in trouble. "It's sort of a special girls' thing since Tristan is at his dad's this weekend."

Gaby is so excited for me that she doesn't question my story. Rebecca has two dads and an older brother, so all she can think about is how great a girls trip would be.

"We'll totally figure it out. No one will know you're gone," Rebecca says.

"Line up!" Ms. Garcia calls. I spot Mattie. As she nears the door and Ms. Garcia's clipboard, her face reddens. What is she doing? I watch as she sort of flings a bit of trash to the right. She steps out of the line and chases the fluttering paper right into the grove of trees! I sort through my lunch and find the wrapper from the chopsticks. I hold it up and watch it wave in the breeze. Perfect.

When it's my turn to go inside, I wait for Ms. Garcia to say, "Mercedes Miller." And then I drop the wrapper and get ready to chase it right into our meeting spot.

But it doesn't move. It's caught on a blade of grass. Malik is behind me and he shoves his lunch bag into my back. "Get moving," he grumbles.

Ms. Garcia has her eyes glued to her attendance list. "Seventy-five." I kick the wrapper with the toe of my sneaker and it breaks loose, fluttering on a gust of wind. Malik is just stepping inside by the time I make it to the grove of trees.

Mattie is waiting for me on a wooden bench. *We made it!* she mouths.

Unseen from the leafy shade of our grove of trees, we watch our classmates.

"We have to wait until they're all inside," I whisper. I sit beside Mattie on the bench. It has a plaque: IN MEMORY OF DOLORES WHITMAN, 1909–1986. I read the words on the plaque aloud: "*First woman graduate of Northern Madrone College.* Isn't it strange to think of a time when women didn't go to college?"

Mattie nods. "I'm definitely going to college."

"Yeah, me too. Of course."

"My mom was the first one in her family to go to college. But she says that because I love to read, college will be easy."

"I think if you can do high school, you can do college. Maybe I'll go here. To Northern Madrone."

"That would be cool," Mattie says. "Especially if Francisco Gómez is still teaching here."

I let Mattie's words hang in the air. It's as hard to imagine going to college as it is to imagine meeting our father. From Miss Whitman's bench, we watch the last stragglers march through the door and get counted by Ms. Garcia.

"All set," I say, once they're gone. "Let's go around that way."

We leave Miss Whitman's bench and head away from the science building. The library should be around the next building, according to the campus map. When we turn the corner, we find ourselves in a big grassy lawn rimmed with paths.

"This must be the Quad," Mattie says, heading straight on the sidewalk. She points ahead. "I see the library."

"If we follow the sidewalk, we'll be going the long way." I head for the grass. "Let's cut across over here."

"But . . ." Mattie points to a sign that says PLEASE STAY ON THE SIDEWALK.

I roll my eyes and gesture around us. College students are everywhere, sitting on picnic tables, on beach towels, on stacks of books. They're talking and reading. One person is playing a worn-out guitar. Blankets are spread out under the trees, shoes piled on the grass and their owners lounging. Someone is juggling.

I step around the sign. I don't even have to turn around to know that Mattie is following me. The Quad smells like pine trees and sweat and something sweet like perfume. A woman dances to weird music coming from a small speaker. Her eyes are closed and her arms flow around her like she's a palm tree.

And then I trip on something.

"Careful!"

An orange.

"Sorry!" says the juggler. He has a sack of oranges next to him. "Keep it!"

I pick it up. I toss it in the air and catch it.

"Nice catch," he says. "Want to learn how to juggle?"

"Mercedes," Mattie hisses behind me. "Let's go."

But I don't listen to her. The guy has a little patch of hair on his chin and he's barefoot. I approach his oranges and say, "May I?" He nods and I grab two more.

I toss one orange.

"Great job," says the juggler.

"Mercedes!" Mattie isn't whispering anymore. She tugs on my shirt. I toss the second orange.

"Exactly," says the guy. "Once you get the hang of two, you can add a third eventually."

"Let's GO!"

I toss the third orange.

Mattie stops bugging me and just watches me. Tristan's dad taught me how to juggle after we were at a fair and I asked him why there were only men jugglers. The oranges fly around and around. The bearded guy whistles.

"Either you're a quick learner or you already knew how to do that."

I smile but don't look at him because I'll drop the oranges if I look away. Out of the corner of my eye I can see him juggling, too. He's doing tricks. At first, Mattie is our only spectator, but then a little audience of college students crowd around us. I am literally the center of attention. They laugh and clap. I'm not sure if my face is warm from the sun that has just popped out from behind a cloud or from the glorious feeling of performing for these people. Me and the oranges and the spotlight. Everything else fades away like the background of a blurry picture.

"Aw, she's so cute," I hear a young woman say.

Cute?! I drop first one and then all of the oranges.

"You're adorable," says the same voice as I kneel. The

oranges are like Easter eggs in the green grass. I turn and see a student in cropped jeans and a flannel shirt. I glare at her. This is all her fault. "I write for the college newspaper. Can I take a picture of you? What's your name? How long have you been juggling?"

I open my mouth to answer. I love talking about myself. I have a lot of practice.

Then the newspaper woman adds, "Where's your mom or dad?"

Dad?

"Mercedes!" Mattie appears from behind the woman.

What am I doing? Performing can wait. Finding Frank Gómez can't.

"Sorry, lady," Mattie says. "We gotta go." For once, I'm relieved when she grabs my arm. She pulls me through the crowd, toward the library.

CHAPTER 27

Mattie

A musty smell attacks us the moment we step inside the brown brick library. We walk past the checkout desk, where a girl with dyed-black hair and a nose ring has a thick book open on the counter. The library is a hush of quiet, especially after the noise of Mercedes's audience. Groups of students are bent over, heads down at the tables. Constellations of dust dance silently in a beam of light shining through the high windows. No sign of a Colombian professor.

"You look that way; I'll look this way," I whisper. I point to the rows of books on each side of the reading room.

How will we find Francisco Gómez? Will we recognize him? In the photo on my dresser, he has scruffy black hair, light-brown skin, a wide nose. His brown eyes have flecks of amber.

We split up and pace—well, run the aisles. My backpack flaps against my back. I can picture it now. I'll come around the end of a row of books and on the other side will be Francisco Gómez. He'll look up from his book and see me. And then he'll recognize me.

Like that first time I saw Mercedes. Her eyes, her nose, her hair. I didn't know her, but I could feel something—something familiar. Francisco Gómez might not realize who I am right away, but he'll know—deep down inside—that a thread connects us.

At least, I hope that's how it works.

"Can I help you?"

I stop in my tracks, one foot in front of the other, and spin around. A woman with brown hair is looking at me over her glasses. She's wearing a brown dress and brown tights and pink combat boots.

"Is there a book emergency?" she asks, and then chuckles. Her large belly jiggles when she laughs and I can't help laughing, too. "Those happen, you know. More often than you might think." She winks at me.

"Uh, I'm not looking for a book. I'm looking for something else."

"Well, then, why don't you come to the reference desk. We'll figure it out."

Before I can answer, she turns. Her ponytail is dyed as bright pink as her boots. She sinks into a chair behind a large wooden desk. A sign above her says: INFORMATION. This is what we need. Information. I finally feel like I'm in the right place.

"Have a seat," she says. She rests her hands flat on the desk and doesn't look at the computer. "I'm Patricia. Patricia Piper, one of the librarians. How can I help you, young lady?" She looks at me like there's nothing else she'd rather do right now than answer my question.

I sit in one of the chairs facing her. "I'm looking for a person, actually."

"Ah, well, I have the internet, phone books, *Who's Who* books."

"He's a professor. Here."

"Ah, that will be simple then. Easy as pie," she says, and snaps her fingers like Mary Poppins.

"What are you doing?" Mercedes appears behind me, literally breathing down my neck where it's ticklish.

"Are you two together?" asks Patricia Piper. "Looking for the same person?"

We nod.

"Well, have a seat, miss," she says, pointing at the other chair. Mercedes sits. "Who are you looking for?"

"Francisco—"

"Frank—"

"Gómez." We finished in unison.

"What a coincidence! Professor Gómez was just here."

The librarian's smiling face goes blurry. The room spins. I feel that invisible thread pulling. This is it. We're going to find him—meet him. Now.

"But, I'm sorry to say, you just missed him."

Mercedes and I both deflate. We missed him again? Tears prick my eyes.

"He was dropping off his book." Patricia Piper reaches under her desk and pulls out a plastic bag. "We love when our visiting professors donate their books to the library. It's so important for students to be able to read the works of their instructors and to have primary source material for their research. Often books by these international professors are difficult to procure in the US. Like this one, never published in America, only in Colombia, Spain, and this copy—the one in English—in Australia." She slides the book out of the bag. "We have to process and catalog it, but you're welcome to look at it."

The book is large, bigger than my seventh-grade math text-book. The cover is swirls in shades of black and the title is in raised white print. *The Seed Sower and Other South American Myths* by Francisco Gómez Flores. I pick it up and the light catches the swirls. I realize that the swirls are pictures. Wolves, panthers, suns, moons, stars, mountains, monkeys. The more I find, the more I see.

"Go ahead," Patricia Piper says, "take it over to that table. Just bring it back when you're done."

"Did he say where he was going?" Mercedes asks.

"He's probably going to the monthly faculty meeting."

Mercedes and I both leap from our chairs.

Patricia Piper laughs. "It's no rush, girls. You can catch him when it's over at one thirty."

"Where?"

"Oh, well, I suppose it's at Madrone Hall. That's the only place that fits all the faculty at once."

The large clock at the end of the reading room ticks to twelve thirty. Plenty of time.

"Thanks," we say at the same time.

Patricia Piper raises her eyebrows above her glasses. "You must be sisters," she says, and smiles.

Mercedes rolls her eyes. The thread tugs. Sisters. It feels more true out here in the real world, the world away from school, and our moms. The world of this college and this pretty library and this nice librarian—who doesn't ask what two twelve-year-olds are doing alone on a college campus.

CHAPTER 28

Mercedes

I don't want to page through some book. I want to get over to Madrone Hall so we don't miss him again. But Mattie is in a trance. Over a book. I sit across the table from her as she pages through *The Seed Sower*. I mean, it's cool that Frank Gómez wrote a book. And I agree it has a cool cover, but myths just make me think of our social studies project. Which we haven't finished yet. I drum my fingers on the table.

"Look at this," she yelps. "Mercury, Venus, Mars, Jupiter, Saturn. Here's the story of the planets like they talked about at the planetarium. It's Pichcaconqui," she says very slowly.

"Pich-what?"

"Pichcaconqui," she repeats. "It's the name of the planets in . . ."—she turns the page—"Inca mythology. The five wandering stars, they're called. Except, like Ms. Garcia said, there are eight planets."

She turns the book so it faces me. There's a drawing of five little men in the sky. I remember that night camping with Tristan's dad. I remember pointing at the sky and saying to Mom, "Look, there's an *M*." I traced the stars that made a dot-to-dot letter *M*. "For Mercedes."

Mom laughed and Tristan's dad said, "It's not an *M*. It's a

W. That's the constellation Cassiopeia. She was a Greek queen who thought she was more beautiful than anyone else. And she was punished by being put in the sky." Tristan's dad looked at Mom and then winked at me. "But we can call it an *M* if you want."

"Oh, here's the Pleiades story, Mercedes," Mattie says. She stops talking while she reads. "The Maya call them little fistfuls of seeds," she tells me.

"Call what?"

"The Pleiades."

I must have a blank look on my face because she explains. "The Pleiades are my favorite. They're this little cluster of stars way on the edge of the galaxy. They're called the Seven Sisters."

OMG, I would *not* want seven sisters. This half of one is enough for me. I stand up. "Let's go, Mattie."

"Wait, look at this. It's a poem. Why is there a poem? The rest of this book is stories and, I think, maybe just information about the different groups where the stories come from."

I can't help rolling my eyes. I do not care about some poem. But I perch on the edge of the chair next to her. I add foot tapping to my finger drumming.

"It's at the end, after the last chapter." She flips the book closed and then open. "It's written by him."

"The Sky Has Many Secrets," she reads aloud.

I remember the one star winking at me. My foot stops tapping.

Mattie reads silently. Her eyes move back and forth across the page, a wrinkle forming above her nose. I know I get the same wrinkle because Tristan always tickles it when I'm reading aloud to him. A chill runs up my spine. She stops reading. She's like stone, like granite. She doesn't say anything but then pushes the book toward me. I don't want to touch it. I don't want to be frozen like Mattie. I want to keep tapping my foot and being annoyed. But I read.

The Sky Has Many Secrets
by Francisco Gómez Flores

I've seen the stars wandering
Across an Amazonian sky
Above the red flames of cooking fire
Over a dusty Andean trail
Beneath the yellow glow of the moon
Goddess
Some nights, the stars
Tell stories of loss
They are the tears of children
Sisters
Daughters of mine
If I could reach across the sky
Would they meet me halfway?

After I read the poem, I read it again. Mattie reads it again, too. Both of us are mouthing the words under our breath. *Amazonian. Moon. Children. Sisters. Daughters.* I don't look at Mattie, but I can feel her next to me, our bodies that look so much alike taking up the same space in this college library. It's weird, but I swear I can feel something—like a thread—connecting us. For a moment, neither of us move. Around us, students are beginning to pack up their books and laptops. They have a Friday kind of energy.

"It's about us," Mattie whispers.

Great, I'm frozen, too. I swallow the annoying lump in my throat. "Maybe, maybe not." I try to sound as breezy as possible, but the lump makes my voice crack. "I mean, poems are weird like that."

But I know that poems tell the stories they're meant to tell. My English teacher last year told me that I had a gift. She loved my poems. It's easy to write a poem. You just put words on the page, words that pop into your brain, words that rearrange themselves in the air before you write them down and somehow, they mean something—maybe something you meant to say and maybe something completely different—to the person reading them. Like your teacher.

Or your daughters.

"What . . . ," Mattie begins. "I mean, why . . ." She turns to me as if I have the answers, but all I have is questions.

Why did Frank Gómez write a poem about his daughters? Why did he put it in some myth book that no one would ever read? Why didn't he write it and send it in an email? Or even on paper, in an envelope? Why didn't he say these words to us in person?

I rub my eyes with clenched fists. Too much dust. I slam the book shut. The sound echoes in the quiet library. "We have to go."

Mattie nods but doesn't move.

"Now."

"I know." Mattie stands up, tears in her eyes. She nods, wipes her nose with the back of her hand. Gross.

"If we want answers, we have to find him."

"I know, I know. I'm coming." She slings on her backpack and then picks up *The Seed Sower*. The animals and shapes appear and disappear on the cover. "It's just so beautiful," she sighs. She hugs the book to her chest. She sniffles. One tear slips down her cheek.

I glance around. The reading room is cleared out; only one student sits at a table in the back. Patricia Piper, with her weird clothes and funny hair, is nowhere to be seen. I unclench my fists and make a choice.

"Put it in your backpack," I say, nodding at the book.

CHAPTER 29

Mattie

s we hurry across the Quad, I feel like every student reading and talking and juggling can tell that I'm a thief. Even though *The Seed Sower* isn't very heavy, my backpack weighs on my back, making my shoulders ache. Or maybe it's just the guilt.

I've never stolen anything in my life. Not a toy from day care, not a candy bar at a gas station, not a pen from a teacher, not even a sugar pack from a restaurant. (Okay, I borrowed Kenny's pocketknife, but I returned it the very next day.) I imagine how the person would feel, knowing someone stole from them, and that stops me. Because I know how bad I would feel if I were missing something, if someone took something of mine.

But *The Seed Sower* is like a magnet and I'm the fridge. It won't let go of me and I can't let go of it. If it were an ordinary book, I would just write down the title and get my own copy. But Patricia Piper said it wasn't the kind of book you could get in the United States. Not anywhere in this whole country. And it was written by Francisco Gómez. And it has a poem. A poem, I'm certain, he wrote for me. For me and Mercedes. So it's my poem, and the poem is in the book, and doesn't that kind of make the book mine?

"According to the map, Madrone Hall is across the road." Mercedes has her rumpled campus map in her hand. "We can cut through that building." She points across the lawn.

She's so certain, I let her lead the way—which turns out to be a very bad idea.

The building we've entered isn't a shortcut at all because we immediately get lost. There are dead-end corridors and half staircases with locked doors at the tops and bottoms. We keep circling back to a small, empty waiting room near a door marked ADMISSIONS. Each time we take a different turn but end up in the same place. The same blue and orange chairs. The same rack of brochures. The same reception desk that has a sign that says PLEASE RING BELL FOR SERVICE.

"We're going to have to ask someone for help," I whisper. I already know that Mercedes is not the kind of person who likes to ask anyone for anything. "Or go back the way we came."

"Let's try this door." She turns the knob of a door marked NO ADMITTANCE.

Before I can stop her, we're in a small office. Walkie-talkies hang from a pegboard. There's a desk. Three telephones. A bowl of yellow butterscotch candies that remind me that I didn't eat my lunch. And on the wall behind the desk is a campus map— like the one we have but more detailed.

"Now what?" I say.

"Now we—"

I can feel him behind me even before I turn around. When I do, I see a walkie-talkie clipped to a belt. A shiny name badge clipped to a crisp white shirt that says, *Darryl, Northern Madrone College Campus Security.*

"Can I help you?"

The man has a thick mustache. His cheeks are red and he's very, very tall.

Mercedes slowly retreats. "We're just, uh, looking for our, uh, cousin."

Even I can tell that's a terrible lie. I back up.

"We'll be going now," she says.

"Hold on, girls." Darryl pulls a notepad from his pocket. "Names?"

"You—you don't need our names," Mercedes says. "We're leaving. Sorry to disturb."

"Sit." He points at a row of three wooden, straight-backed chairs.

There's something about the way he says it that makes me nervous. And makes Mercedes obey. We sit.

"Who are you here to visit?"

"Um," says Mercedes.

"You're not runaways from the Poppy View field trip, are you?" The security guard's bushy eyebrows scrunch together. "You wouldn't be the first." He unhooks the walkie-talkie from his belt. "I can notify the teachers in two seconds." He sounds like he would actually *like* to get us in trouble. "Ask if they're missing two girls?"

Black spots appear in front of my eyes. There's a faint buzzing in my ears. A migraine? A panic attack? *Panic episode*, I hear my mom say.

"Like we said, we're visiting our cousin," Mercedes says.

"Oh, really? And what's her name?"

Ten, nine, eight, seven.

"Samantha," Mercedes says

"Betty?" I say at the same time.

Maybe if we were full sisters, not half sisters, we would have made up the same fake name.

"Listen," Darryl says. He crouches down in front of us so we're eye to eye. "Two little girls should not be wandering around a college campus." He looks back and forth. Me, Mercedes, me. "It could be dangerous."

He's right. Anything could be a risk. Or life changing. You don't know by just looking. The maze at the apple orchard didn't seem scary until I got lost. When my mom first met Bob, I had no idea that everything I knew would transform completely. What will change because Mercedes and I decided to sneak away and look for our father? Maybe Darryl is a sign that we should just go back to the planetarium, slip in next to November and Sunny, pretend like this never happened. Pretend we never tried to find Francisco Gómez. Pretend we don't know who that is. Why did I listen to Mercedes? *Five, four, three.* I try to slow my breathing.

"We're not *little*." Mercedes's voice is more firm now.

"I just want to make sure you get where you belong."

I wish Darryl—or anyone—could tell us where that was.

"We know where we're going," Mercedes insists. "We're visiting our sister. Honest."

"You said cousin."

"We did?" Mercedes looks at me and laughs like she doesn't have a care in the world. "How silly. We're visiting our sister."

"And your sister has two different names?"

"Yeah," Mercedes says quickly. Like she's relearning how to

tell a good story. "She does, actually. I mean, *we* call her Betty, but everyone else calls her Sarah."

I nudge Mercedes. "Or Samantha."

"Is she a child prodigy?" the security guard says.

"Oh, no," I say, "she's a lot older than us."

"She's finishing a test," Mercedes continues, "in quantum physics." How does she even know that word?

"Not many Mexicans in physics."

"We're not Mexican." Her cheeks are turning red and she clenches her fists. I can feel the anger radiating off of her like she's one of those stars in the planetarium, shining extra bright so you can see her.

"Is that so?" he says.

Mercedes squints at him. Her eyes are lasers.

"Colombian," I say automatically. I'm so used to correcting people who assume I'm Mexican. Or Filipino. Or Native American. Never Colombian. Looking at myself in the mirror—or at Mercedes—it's obvious by the shape of my nose, the color of my hair, the angle of my cheeks that I'm *something*. And so I always correct them. Colombian, I always say. Even though I know nothing about Colombia, speak no Spanish, and don't even know my own Colombian father.

"Not many women in physics, either." Darryl walks behind the desk, turns to the wall, reaches out a finger and runs it along a list of names and phone numbers posted beside the map. "It'll be easy to see if you're telling the truth," he mumbles as he scans the list, hand on his walkie-talkie at his hip. "Physics department," he reads. It's just enough time for Mercedes to grab my arm and pull me back through the No Admittance door.

As if guided by unseen superpowers, this time we make it through the maze-like hallways and out of the building. As we run, my backpack and the stolen book inside slap against me, reminding me of all the rules I've broken today. We burst through a heavy windowless door. A back entrance. Every inch of my body feels like it did on the Speeding Saucers. Dizzy. Excited. Scared. Happy. I check to see if the security guard is following us. But the metal door stays firmly shut.

"That was close!"

"We should get our story straight," Mercedes says, and grins. She doesn't mind breaking rules. In fact, it looks like she enjoys it.

"What the heck is quantum physics?"

"I'm not sure," Mercedes says with a shrug. "But Tristan watches a lot of Discovery Channel."

"My stepbrother Lucas is obsessed with dinosaurs."

"I went through a dinosaur phase," Mercedes says. "How about you?"

"No, I was more into horses."

"Typical girl stuff?"

I laugh. "I guess so. I wanted to be a princess who rode horses."

"Too bad that's not a career option." Mercedes giggles. "I wanted to be a ninja princess."

"We could have been a team—the two princesses that ride horses and fight bad guys."

We laugh again, but this time it feels like a sad laugh. We'll never know if we would have been sisters who played princess together. The thread that tugs between us feels so fragile.

"Well, come on, princess," Mercedes says after a moment. We follow the footpath that leads from the door through a cluster of shrubs. The air is crisp, maybe like an Andean trail. We duck under another grove of trees and then—like a miracle— we're at the road.

According to the campus map, Madrone Hall should be straight ahead.

And there it is. A white building with a staircase that reminds me of the entrance to the palace in Cinderella. A big sign in neat, round letters says MADRONE HALL. Mercedes doesn't bother to look both ways but pulls me by my backpack straps across the road. "We made it."

This is it. I stand at the bottom of the Cinderella steps. The building is fancier and newer looking than the others on campus. It has iron scrolls around the windows and a red roof. And our father is inside. A car drives past, making a clanking noise as it goes. A clump of students, each in ripped jeans, walks toward the parking lot.

I don't know what a faculty meeting is, but it sounds important. My father, Francisco Gómez, is a person who goes to important meetings. And we're going to meet him. I don't know if I should be excited or scared or worried. All I do know is that this is one of the strangest days of my life. I squeeze my eyes shut and then open. No more black spots. I want to remember this moment forever, the moment before I meet my father. Beside me, Mercedes inhales like she's about to say something. But she's silent. Maybe she doesn't know how to feel, either.

Together, we climb the stairs to the entrance of Madrone Hall.

· · ·

I was the bridesmaid in my mom's wedding. While Bob waited for the ceremony to begin, he kept pulling on his coat sleeves. I walked down the aisle after Lucas and Kenny, who stood by their dad. Last came my mom. I remember watching her walking toward us. She didn't wear a veil, but she had tiny daisies in her hair. She smiled at the guests—our friends and a few cousins, plus Bob's family members who had flown in from California. As she walked, the aisle in the backyard seemed to stretch longer and longer, and it felt like she would never arrive. I watched my mom and knew this was the moment that everything would change forever.

I know that this is another moment that can change everything. The steps to the entrance of Madrone Hall seem as endless as that aisle. But, at last, Mercedes and I reach the big glass doors.

She pulls.

"Locked?!" she screeches.

She yanks. She screams. All four of the doors at the entrance to Madrone Hall are locked. I press my face against the windowpane and shield the light with my hands. Inside the big open lobby is another set of doors that are also closed. Light streams in from a skylight. No faculty. No meeting. No students. Just a big, empty space. Empty as my heart feels.

Mercedes keeps pulling and pushing on the handles, first one, then the other. Then she kicks the doors, first one, then the other.

"We probably missed them because of the security guard," she says. "It's his fault!"

"Where is he?" I ask. She knows I'm not talking about the security guard. And she knows that I know that she doesn't know. And that I don't know what else to say.

"Why did we even come here? This is your fault!" Mercedes glares at me.

"It was your idea!"

She pounds on the locked doors with her fists, and then she kicks them with the rubber toe of her sneaker. Then she kicks a potted plant near the doors, a pile of dry leaves at the edge of the staircase, a sign that says NO SMOKING. She's screaming, too. I realize she's not screaming at me—she just needs to spit out words. Nonsense. Nothing makes sense. Not her screaming, not her kicking. Not the security guard, not the search for a man we've never met. I sit down on the steps as far from her kicking as I can get. What now?

"Patricia Piper," she says like the librarian's name tastes bad. "She lied to us." She kicks the door again, yanks on the handle. "I'm glad we took that book. Serves her right."

The book in my backpack feels unbearably heavy. I plop down on the top step and sling the bag off my shoulders. I close my eyes, blocking out Mercedes's kicking, wishing I could block out her yelling. When I open them, a man with a gray beard and sunglasses is walking up the steps, two at a time.

"Can I help you?"

Mercedes stops kicking and spins around. She pants. I stand up and put my arm around her shoulders. Her face is red.

"Hi," I say to the man. "Everything's fine." My voice sounds froggy. I clear my throat. "We thought there was a faculty meeting here. We were supposed to meet . . ." I pause and think for a second. "We're supposed to meet our aunt."

"Yes, our aunt," agrees Mercedes.

"It seems you've been misinformed by your aunt," the man says. "The faculty meeting was last Friday. Once a month. I'm here to unlock the hall for the concert tonight."

Mercedes and I look at each other. I can tell what she's thinking: she's extra glad we stole the book.

"Can I help you find your aunt? Or call someone for you?" the man asks, his brushy gray eyebrows getting even bushier with concern.

"No," I say as quickly and breezily as I can before he offers to call the security guard. "We'll just go to her office. We know where it is."

I grab Mercedes's hand and pull her down the steps.

CHAPTER 30

Mercedes

om says my temper tantrums are proof that I'll be a great CEO someday. Not that I'd ever want to have a job like hers, always traveling, always working, never home. But she means I have a lot of energy and that I care. But sometimes I wish I didn't care so much. When Mom first started traveling for work, I used to have major tantrums. Kicking—like I just did—and screaming. I would hide her purse, dump out her travel-sized bottles of shampoo. But, of course, it didn't help. She still left. Every time.

Now Mattie drags me away from Madrone Hall. My tantrum didn't do anything except stub my big toe. In fact, the person my temper hurts the most is usually me. A sore throat from screaming, a bruised arm from hitting something, humiliation when someone sees me.

I'm embarrassed now. Mattie has just witnessed a full-blown Mercedes Miller Tantrum. Gaby and Rebecca are both used to seeing me lose it. Cristina hardly flinches. Mom just tells me about my future life as an executive. The only person who seems to be bothered by my outbursts is Tristan. He hugs me, even when I'm yelling. Because he's younger than me, I know I need to be a better example.

"Feel better?" Mattie asks when we get to the road.

I shrug.

"Maybe take a few deep breaths. That always helps me."

I stare at her. I want to lash out again. I want to yell and tell her it's none of her business. But she stares at me like it doesn't bother her that I had a major fit. My lungs fill with the woodsy air. I can smell the ocean and burnt popcorn and car exhaust. I pull my phone out of my pocket and check the time. "We've got twenty minutes before Ms. Garcia leads the troops back to school."

"Come on," Mattie says. "Let's take a walk. We both need to calm down before we go back."

Part of me—the old Mercedes?—wants to tell her that I don't need to calm down and that she's not the boss of me, but instead I follow her across the street and along the path toward the middle of campus. We avoid the science building and don't talk about missing Frank Gómez again or the stupid librarian or the fact that our field trip is over.

We duck under the madrone trees and end up on the other side of the athletic complex. Mattie stops at the fence that overlooks the Olympic-sized swimming pool below.

Neither of us say anything. The water sparkles in the sun.

"What time is it now?" Mattie asks.

I look at my phone. "It's two thirty."

"We should probably sneak back into the planetarium. The buses are leaving at two forty-five."

I don't answer at first, just stare at the water sparkling in the sun. An idea is slowly forming. "What if we don't?"

"Don't what?"

"What if we don't go back with them?" I turn to face Mattie. I look into her brown eyes. "I'm serious. What if we stay and keep looking for Frank Gómez? We have the bus schedule." I gesture at her backpack. "We have one on my phone and one in there."

"What about when I don't come home from school? My mom will be so worried."

I think about *my* mom. She won't be worried because she's not home. She's never home. But I bat away thoughts of her. I say, "I have a plan." I know Mattie loves plans. "We're going to track him down, even if it takes all night."

"We can't stay here all night! At Northern Madrone? I don't have my toothbrush!"

"It probably won't come to that. Don't worry." I tell her we just need to give ourselves a little time, a bit of wiggle room to find Frank Gómez. I show her the transit schedule: there's a bus at 4:20 and a final bus at 6:15.

"Are you sure it will work to take the city bus home?"

"Yes, Mattie, I'm sure. It'll be fine." I'm already texting Cristina, telling her that I'm sleeping over at Mattie's house. Cristina responds with an offer to pick me up in the morning, but I text that I'll call. No need to tell her yet that she might have to pick us up from Northern Madrone College.

"This will never work."

"Here." I hand Mattie my phone. "Just tell your mom you're sleeping over at my house. Like last weekend. She'll think we're besties."

She holds the phone like it's a grenade. Her face looks a little green.

"It'll work. Don't panic." Ugh, that's the last thing I need right now. She needs to hold it together, and I can't get mad. *We* need to hold it together.

"We already talked about this—this kind of thing only works in movies."

"Trust me, Mat."

She must decide to trust me because she enters the number. "Mama?" she says.

I look away. Give her some privacy for her lie. Not that I'm worried. I'm sure she can do it. All those people asking if they can help us, all those answers we gave them. She's been practicing for this lie all day.

"Oh, hi, Bob," Mattie says haltingly. "Is my mom there?" She looks at me and mouths, *My stepdad answered my mom's phone.* I would be so mad if I were her. But Mattie just says, "Okay. Can you ask her if I can sleep over at my friend Mercedes's house? You know, like I did last week?" She's quiet, listening to whatever Bob is saying. "No, she doesn't need to pick me up. I'm going home with her right after school. No, she can loan me some pajamas. Yes, I'll tell them." She listens again. "Uh, okay."

She hands me back my phone. It's warm from the call. She looks stunned. "I snuck out of school and stole a book and got in trouble with a security guard and lied to my mom and my new stepdad."

"It's not a lie," I reassure her. "It's a . . . story."

She glares at me as if it were my fault. "I've never done any of those things before. And I never wanted to," she adds.

"Think about this. If we didn't lie, your mom would worry.

And Cristina could lose her job. And the teachers would get in trouble. We're just keeping everyone safe—keeping them happy—by telling a not-so-true story."

"I suppose."

She looks resigned but not pleased. I check my phone. It's two forty-five. We need to find him before he goes home. Grown-ups usually work until five or six. Mom works until eight or nine at night, but she's a workaholic. I don't know if Frank Gómez is, but if it means we'll be able to find him, I won't mind.

"Ready?" I ask.

"I think I need a minute after all that lying."

Mattie leans on the chain-link fence and stares down at the pool below. The entire pool area is deserted, the bleachers empty, the gates padlocked. I pull out my phone again and snap a selfie. My hair is backlit by the sun glittering on the pool water.

Mattie watches me and then says, "We need a picture of us together."

"We do?"

"Here we are, on the search for our dad. Telling lies. It's momentous."

Momentous failure, I think. But I hold out my phone at arm's length. "Get in," I command, leaning toward her.

Mattie stares at the camera with a goofy grin. The trees behind us make a perfect backdrop. If only she knew how to take a selfie. "Don't you know how to pose?" I tilt my head and press my cheek against hers. Her curls tickle my face. She attempts the tilt, but I can't help laughing at her ridiculous expression displayed on the screen. "We need a better angle." I lean way forward, rest one arm on the fence, and snap a picture. The green leaves of the madrones behind us look brilliant in the sunlight. "Okay, one more. Can't you, like, lean back a little?"

She tries to lean back, angle her head, press her cheek. "Um, is that better?"

"Well, no." I can't quite get the right shot of us. And it feels suddenly like the most important thing in the world to get this photo perfect. Like, if we can't find Frank Gómez, at least we'll have proof that we tried—together. I lean even farther over the fence that overlooks the pool, stretch my arm. The light is perfect. If I can just—

And then, in what feels like slow motion, my fingers slip. I yelp. I reach. I flail. The phone falls like a shooting star, the shiny case glinting in the sun. It bounces off the rocks and exposed dirt of the steep hillside beyond the fence. Bits of plastic fly in different directions. What is left of my phone then clatters to the pool deck, teeters for a moment on the edge, and then, as if pushed by some magical force, plunges into the blue water below.

Mattie gasps. "Uh-oh."

We watch the small rectangle sink to the bottom of the pool.

"NO!" I scramble, put one foot into the chain link. Maybe I can climb over the fence. Mattie grabs the back of my sweatshirt. "Get down!"

"Mattie!" I swirl around. "This is all your fault!"

"What?" she hollers back.

"If you weren't such a dork, you'd know how to take a sel-fie! I wouldn't have had to lean out so far. I never would have dropped my phone!"

"You're the one who dropped it. And if you would have followed the rules like I did, you wouldn't even have your phone!"

"Exactly!" I'm breathing hard, can hardly catch my words. Mattie backs up like she's a little afraid of me. "You couldn't do any of this without me." I wave my arms at, well, at all of Northern Madrone College. She wouldn't be here if it weren't for me.

"This was *our* plan, not just yours." Mattie puts her hands on her hips. "We're in this together."

"Yeah. Together without a phone." I want to stomp and scream some more, but two Mercedes Miller Tantrums in one afternoon is too much, even for me. I grab onto Mattie's shoulders and stare into her eyes. *My* eyes. I'm so mad my hands are shaking. I say very slowly, "What are we supposed to do now, huh, Miss Plan Ahead Matilde?"

She shakes loose. "Let me think." Mattie paces, avoids looking over the fence at the useless scrap of technology lying on the bottom of the pool. "We don't have a phone, but that's okay, because we already called home. We'll catch the city bus. Aren't you glad for Operation D.A.D? At least I kept the schedule."

I cross my arms over my chest. She's right. I *am* glad for the old-fashioned Santa Cruz Transit schedule in her backpack. My breathing slows.

This time it's Mattie who says, "You have to trust me, okay?"

I inhale. "Okay, fine. I trust you." Mostly because I don't have much of a choice.

"Now we have to figure out how to find him. And not lose him again."

Mattie says the only choice we have is to return to the anthropology department and wait for him. Be *patient*. Boring! But she's right; we can't keep moving from place to place or we'll miss him again. And we need to stay out of sight of the security guard.

"And no more listening to nice librarians," I say. I decide right then and there that we're not trusting any more adults here. So far none of them has helped us even though they keep asking if they can. It's obvious that they can't.

From now on, it's just the two of us—me and Mattie.

CHAPTER 31

Mattie

L osing Mercedes's phone makes us more determined than ever. We head toward the now-familiar route back to the Humanities building, but just as we turn away from the athletic complex, we run into a crowd of forty or fifty students gathered on the sidewalk.

"What's going on?" I ask Mercedes.

The college students' faces are painted with swirling blue-and-green earths, with rainbows, with peace signs. They carry cardboard placards on wooden stakes. THERE IS NO PLANET B. EARTH IS OUR ONLY HOPE. STOP DRILLING THE ARCTIC.

"What do we want?" shouts a guy through a megaphone.

"Clean energy to save the planet!" answers the crowd.

"When do we want it?"

"Now!"

We back up onto the grass and observe, listening to their chants, reading their signs. "It's a protest march," Mercedes tells me.

"Did you know only ten percent of campus energy comes from clean fuels?" a student with many multicolored braids in her hair shouts at us. She's wearing a long dress and sandals and has about a hundred woven bracelets on her wrists. "Would you like to sign our petition?" She thrusts a clipboard into my hands. She smells weird and I back up a little.

"You want *our* signatures?" Mercedes asks.

"We're just kids," I add.

"We need the young people," the braid woman says. "Do you girls know that you're our future?"

"I guess."

"We're petitioning for a second wind turbine and to mandate that fifty percent of energy used comes from the turbines. And we need all the signatures we can get."

I don't know what wind turbines and energy-use percentages mean, but we both sign the petition, adding our names under the completely illegible signatures of the college students who signed before me.

The crowd gets bigger, and now college students bump our elbows as they continue down the sidewalk toward the parking lot. As we watch from our spot in the grass, Mercedes says, "I saw a protest march from my mom's office in San Francisco last year. She's on the fourteenth floor, but even from up there you could see all the signs. 'Black Lives Matter' and 'No Justice, No Peace.' Stuff like that. It's pretty great to see people standing up for what they believe in."

"That's so cool." And then I admit, "Protests—well, crowds—makes me nervous. I get anxious sometimes."

Mercedes just nods as if she already figured that out.

"When I go to college," I say as the students turn into a river of people all heading in the same direction, "I'm definitely going to go to protests."

"Mat," she says, grinning. "We're already at college. Why not start today?"

I try to protest against Mercedes's idea of joining the protest. It's one thing to imagine doing it when I'm older, and another to actually try it now. I don't like yelling and I don't like fighting. *Mattie doesn't like conflict*, my mom always says.

That's been the strangest part about living with stepbrothers—all their conflict. Even though they're five years apart, it seems like they fight all the time. Kenny kicks Lucas under the dining room table. Lucas sticks out his tongue at Kenny in the back seat of my mom's new minivan. They argue about playing chess with me—even though Lucas doesn't even know how. They fight over the remote, an old basketball, even a fluffy blue blanket.

"Give it!" Kenny yelled at his brother the first night at the rented cabin in Minnesota when Bob made us watch a movie together. *Moana*. It was the only one that our whole brand-new family could agree on.

"You two need to share," Bob said.

While I watched from an old rocking chair in the corner, Kenny grabbed the blanket out of Lucas's hands. "Ha!" he gloated. "Got it." Then he saw the warning look from his dad. "Sit by me, Lukey, and I'll share." Kenny patted the spot on the couch next to him. Lucas, from his slump on the floor in front of the TV, eyed his brother like he didn't trust him. At last, Lucas got up and snuggled next to Kenny under the blanket. Bob smiled at my mom like he was parent of the year. It seemed like the sharing was going to work.

But just when Moana heads out to sea, Lucas started pinching Kenny. Then Kenny punched Lucas on the thigh. Then Lucas cried. Kenny swatted his head and told him to cut it out. And then both of them were sent to bed. They both missed out on the ice cream after the movie, which Bob says is part of the family movie night experience. As I ate my mint chip, I thought about how it seemed like it would be easier if they would just get along.

"Come on, Mattie," Mercedes says, her eyes sparkling. "It'll be fun."

"What about finding Francisco Gómez? We're supposed to go wait for him at the Humanities building."

"We'll find him," Mercedes says confidently.

"I thought we needed to focus!"

"A little detour won't hurt. We have plenty of time before the 4:20 bus." She raises her voice to be heard above the crowd. "Come on!"

There's something about her that makes it very hard to say no to her.

I get swept along with Mercedes and the protest. College students and their cardboard signs surround me. "Wait up!" I loop my elbow through hers. I'm not losing her in this crowd.

We follow as the protest marches along the sidewalk past the library. The stolen book slaps against my back like a code saying, *Guilty*. Faces peer out at us from the windows above like an audience. I'm grateful that Mercedes doesn't let go of my elbow. We pass the student union, where we earn a few whoops from the onlookers. We turn the corner past the science building and the planetarium. Guilt knocks against me again as I think about my mom, who has no idea I'm at a protest at Northern Madrone College.

All around us, the chanting of voices makes me feel like I'm stuck in a wind tunnel of noise. "What do we want?" the man with the megaphone shouts. "When do we want it?"

"Clean energy to save the planet!" Mercedes's voice projects above the shouting. But I'm afraid my voice won't carry. I think about the riddle—if a tree falls in a forest and there's no one to hear it, does it make a sound? Does my voice do anything if no one—not even me—can hear it? How will I know if braving this crowd has been worth it? What story will I tell about this day?

The marchers circle the parking lot and take up the whole road. A maroon car is caught in the crowd, inching along with the people walking. The back bumper is plastered with stickers. FOLLOW ME TO THE LIBRARY. MYSTERY SPOT SANTA CRUZ. PEACE BEGINS AT HOME. RESPECT NATURE. DON'T BELIEVE EVERYTHING YOU THINK. A trail of fingerprints in the dust has left stripes on the shiny doors. I reach out and touch the smooth metal, adding my own fingerprint. "What do we want?" I hear from up ahead. There's something about the crowd, the man's voice, the stickers on the car. Somehow, while touching the smooth steel of the car, I feel brave. Strong. I feel the energy bubbling up from my toes, up to my knees, my chest. And I yell.

"Clean energy to save the planet!" I chant. And then I yell again and again along with the crowd. My throat gets raw with shouting. Mercedes's voice next to me is an echo, her words coming just a fraction of a second behind mine. Together, but different. It feels good to hear my own voice.

And then I hear another.

"Great job, kids. Glad to see you taking action."

It's the driver of the car. Her window is open and she's grinning at us. The woman's gray hair is cut in a short, straight style. She's wearing huge sunglasses—even though it's not that sunny—studded with sparkly, rainbow-colored gems. We're surrounded by student protesters, but the woman is looking right at me and Mercedes like she's our fairy godmother or something.

"Good for you, girls. If you want something bad enough, you have to believe in it and then work really hard for it. You can't let it out of your focus." She winks as she sneaks her car forward, escaping through a break in the crowd.

Mercedes and I both stop walking and watch her drive away. The marchers weave around us like we're rocks in a stream. Pretty soon we're standing alone in the middle of the road. When a car honks, we scurry to the sidewalk.

You can't let it out of your focus. The words echo in my head. I look at Mercedes. I'm pretty sure they're echoing in her head, too. The thread between us tugs on a place deep in my heart.

"Are you thinking what I'm thinking?" I ask as we watch the protest disappear around a bend in the road.

"That we should keep looking for him?"

I nod. "Which way is his office?"

When we arrive at Francisco Gómez's office door, it's still closed. Locked. We slump against the wall and slide to the floor. "We'll wait," I say.

"Where *is* he?" Mercedes whines. "This is so annoying."

"Can I help you?" The woman in the blue dress that we saw earlier is glaring down at us. She doesn't look like she wants to see us much less to help us.

I scramble to my feet. "We're looking for Francisco Gómez. Someone said he was here."

She checks her watch. "Well, it's quarter to four. He must be teaching his last class." She pulls her green fleece jacket closer around her.

"We missed him again?" Mercedes isn't talking to the woman, she's looking at me.

"Do you know where his class is?" I ask politely.

"You can't just show up at a college class, you know, girls."

"We know. We just need to tell him something. Our, um, teacher has a message for him. Super important."

I don't know where these stories are coming from, but they seem to be working. The woman looks at me and then at Mercedes like she doesn't trust us. I don't blame her. My stomach clenches from all the lies.

Finally, she says, "The Morgan Lecture Hall in the biology building."

CHAPTER 32

Mercedes

M y legs burn as we race from the Humanities building. Toward our father. We can't lose any more time; we can't get distracted. Mattie's right behind me as I run down the sloping sidewalk. It feels so good to just move, to pump my legs, to feel the burn in my chest.

Following the directions the woman gave us, we head past the athletic complex again, and neither of us even glances at the pool. We go through the grove of eucalyptus. We pass the perfect black oval of the track, where five or six people in shorts and tanks are even faster than we are. As I run up the grassy hill as instructed; I slow down so Mattie can catch up. Ahead of us is the building, just like the woman said it would be—two stories of brick and stone.

With a sign out front that says HEALTH SCIENCES.

"Where's the biology building?" Mattie asks. As if I know. "Isn't this where she told us to go? 'Follow the sidewalk past the pool, past the track, through the trees, and up the hill'?"

Those were the exact instructions. *You can't miss it*, the woman with the hopeless fashion sense said. So why wasn't this the biology building? We pull out the campus map, but there are no buildings labeled biology.

"Maybe it's on the other side." I stretch my calves and then circle the building.

The rear of the Health Sciences building faces the woods. A dirt path disappears into the trees. The stench of dead leaves and mold tickles my nose.

Mattie sneezes. "Just a second. I need a tissue," she says. She stops and digs in her backpack. "Aha! Operation D.A.D. to the rescue!" I roll my eyes. "What's that?" she asks as she blows her nose, pointing behind a tall shrub dotted with pink flowers.

Instead of brick, the back corner of the building is two stories of glass. The panes are clouded with steam, little rivulets of water leaving snaking paths like escape routes. Mammoth leaves, yellow flowers, red branches press against the windows. A glass door is propped open with a big stone.

"It's a greenhouse," I say, heading for the door.

"I don't think we're supposed to go in there, Mercedes."

Mattie is always so nervous.

"Why did they leave the door open, then?"

"We need to keep moving," she says. But she follows me anyway.

Walking into the greenhouse is like entering a different country. I know we need to focus, but I can't help myself. A thick green scent hangs in the air. The cement floor is damp with puddles. Black plastic pots as big as bathtubs hold huge trees, some familiar looking and some covered in strange fruit—yellow, green, orange. Some have leaves bigger than my head. One has branches that droop like it's the saddest tree in the world. In the middle of the room are tables buried in more plants. Tall grassy ones, short flowering ones. One is a vine with black leaves. Each plant or tree has a little metal sign with labels. *Cattleya trianae. Streptosolen jamesonii. Heliconia bihai.* I reach out and touch a velvety leaf. *Setaria palmifolia. Plumeria rubra.* Mom would love it in here. She loves plants. Her babies. When her plumeria blooms, she tells me to smell them. "Really get in there, Mercedes," Mom says. "Get your nose close and breathe it in."

"Look at this one," Mattie calls as I bend down to smell a rich red flower with spiky yellow leaves.

I join her at the other end of the long table. The plant has tall narrow leaves and strange yellow blobs. I suppose they're flowers, but they look like cobs of yellow corn. Or snakeskin. *Calathea crotalifera.* A second label is in English: RATTLESNAKE PLANT.

"Yikes." Maybe I shouldn't touch anything in here. I wipe my hand on my jeans.

"What *is* this place?" Mattie asks, looking up, around. She's mesmerized by the green and the thick air and the colors.

"A greenhouse. A conservatory. It must be for studying plants," I say. "I could stay here forever."

"It smells like heaven," Mattie says. She plops down on a green metal bench and lifts her face, closing her eyes and soaking in the smells.

"My mom loves plants." I think of her plants and then I think of her company that's all about computers and data and numbers and codes. "She should have become a florist or something. Not a tech person."

Mattie doesn't say anything. She strokes a fuzzy green leaf the size of her palm. It's nice when someone just listens. "What do you want to be?"

I shrug. "I don't know. I want to be someone onstage. An actor? How about a movie star?"

"You could be a juggler." She giggles.

"I'm pretty good, aren't I? What do you want to be?"

"I want to be the person who leads you around a museum, telling you about the art or the old maps or whatever. Is that a job?"

I shake my head. "I don't know, Mattie." I picture her walking through a museum. "I hope so because you would be good at that. You're good at explaining things."

"I'm glad I don't have to decide yet."

I stand beside her. A peaceful feeling settles over me like a blanket. The scent, the colors. The green all around us. I feel every inch of my body relaxing, softening. And then a thought fights its way through the warm floral scents filling my brain. I wish I could take this home with me, show Mom.

At last I say, "We gotta get out of here, Mattie," even though I don't want to. "Come on."

We drag ourselves up and slip back out the open door. The fresh air of campus clears our heads as we follow the sidewalk. At the front of the building, a woman in jeans and messy bun rushes past. Before I can stop her, Mattie holds out her arm like someone hailing a taxi. "Where's the biology building?" she asks the woman. "The Morgan Lecture Hall?"

"Here," the woman says, pointing at the building.

"But it says Health Science," Mattie says.

The woman nods. "Everyone calls it the biology building. The lecture hall is in there."

I feel *so* stupid. Even though I want to blame the annoying woman in the blue dress, I know it's not her fault. If it's anyone's fault, it's Mom's for liking plants. But at least we're in the right place now.

Mattie swings the front door open and we torpedo inside. The orange carpet of the hushed entrance dampens the sound of our footsteps. Not a student in sight. Mattie points to the left, where an arrow points to a sign that says MORGAN LECTURE HALL.

Is this it? Are we actually going to find Frank Gómez? "Let's go."

We follow the arrow and walk through another set of double doors. Right into a crowd of students.

This crowd isn't loud like the protesters. They're quiet and serious. The carpet mutes their hushed voices as they say things like *qualitative study* and *sociocultural evolution* and *methodological approach.*

"Excuse me," I say, tapping a long-haired girl on the shoulder, "do you know where Frank Gómez's class is?"

She turns and then pulls out her earbuds. "Can I help you?"

"We're looking for Frank—Francisco Gómez."

"His class just ended. I was in it. Great lecture." She puts one earbud back in.

I tug on her purple Northern Madrone sweatshirt. "But do you know where he is?" I feel desperate. We can't have missed him again.

"He usually heads out the other way." She points vaguely and then taps another student on the shoulder. "Hey, Aiden. Did you see which way Professor Gómez went?"

The student stops. "Oh, hi, Kelly."

"They're looking for Professor Gómez," the woman says. "Did you see which way he went?"

Aiden glances at Mattie. "I just talked to him after class and he said he was heading home. If you hurry, maybe you can catch him in the parking lot. He drives a little green Prius," he says to Kelly.

"That fits him so perfectly," Kelly says cheerfully. She does not seem to understand that our life's purpose is about to be ruined.

"The parking lot?" Mattie repeats, looking like someone just threw a bucket of cold water on her. "What's a Prius?"

I feel twitchy all over. "Let's go!"

We run again. Out the door, around the Science and Engineering Building, through the eucalyptus grove, past Miss Whitman's bench. When we reach the parking lot, we watch, panting, as a small car the color of the madrone leaves takes a right. We stand glued to the black asphalt and watch the Prius follow the road through the trees. It shouldn't have been a surprise that after all the searching and the chasing, the only sight we get of Frank Gómez is the tailpipe of his car.

CHAPTER 33

Mattie

I sit on the curb and burst into tears. Nothing and no one—not even Mercedes—is going to stop me from crying. Francisco Gómez is gone. Our chance—probably our only chance ever—to meet our father is gone. Disappeared. I think of the lies—stories, as Mercedes called them—I told my mom and the students and the librarian and the security guard. I think of skipping out of the field trip and missing the green Prius. I think of the stolen book weighing against my back. And for what?

"It's going to be okay," Mercedes says. She sits on the curb next to me, so close her shoulder is touching mine. Her voice is quiet, gentle, but her fists are clenched into tight balls. "It's not our fault."

"What are we going to do?" I ask through my tears. I can't help myself. And I can't stop crying. My hands have gone cold and clammy, and wiping them on my jeans doesn't help. My heart is a ticking time bomb waiting for the moment to explode out of my body. I cover my face with my hands. Even through closed eyes, I see spots of light and red and black. Am I going to faint? *Please*, I think, *please don't let me faint. Please don't let me die.* If my mom were here, she would tell me to breathe. *In. Out.* But I'm so sick of breathing, of trying to calm myself down.

"It's over." My voice is as hard as the concrete curb.

"No," she says firmly. "This isn't over."

"What do you mean?" I ask, my voice shaky like I'm on the Speeding Saucers. I use the edge of my not-so-new T-shirt to wipe my nose. "It *is* over, Mercedes. He's gone. Drove away." I sniff the snot in my nose. "It's over."

"Wait—"

"It's got to be past four twenty. I have no idea how we're getting home!" The thought of my mom thinking I'm safe at Mercedes's house and all the lies I've told is too much. I sob. I don't care what Mercedes thinks of me right now.

She watches me for a moment. Then she sighs and rummages in my backpack.

"Hey—" I protest.

She pulls out the Santa Cruz Transit schedule. The edges of the paper are soggy from a leak in my water bottle. "We're going to get you home. If that's what you need. We'll take the bus home and say we tried." She smooths out the schedule. "We may have missed the four twenty pickup, but we can wait for the six fifteen." She zips up my backpack and hands it to me. "Come on. I saw the bus shelter near Madrone Hall."

She starts walking, certain that I'll follow her.

And I do. I jump off the curb and chase after her. She's right; we see the Santa Cruz Transit bus shelter in a grove of trees near the main entrance to Madrone Hall. We slump on the bench inside. The shelter is made of three plexiglass walls scratched with initials and dirty words. The air is crisp. The sun casts orange shadows on the eucalyptus.

Mercedes folds and unfolds the bus schedule. I don't comment about how she should be glad I kept that paper copy.

"Whenever Tristan loses something," she says after a few moments, "Cristina says that maybe it doesn't want to be found. Maybe Frank Gómez doesn't want to be found."

When I don't answer, she stands up and paces the bus shelter. I feel terrible. Is she giving up on finding Francisco Gómez just because I want to go home? She inspects a spray-painted design of a flower on one wall of the shelter. Then she paces to the other side where there's a posted version of the bus schedule. She stops her pacing and stares at it.

"Um, Mattie?" she says. "Wasn't there supposed to be a bus at six fifteen?"

I nod. "Right. That's the last bus of the day."

"Come here," she says, her voice hollow.

"What?" I leave my backpack on the bench and stand beside her. Together we study the sign.

11:15 AM

2:30 PM

4:20 PM

I scan the rest of the schedule. Where are the other times for Friday? Why are there only three pickup times? All the other weekdays have four pickups.

I hold out the schedule again, compare it to the one on the shelter's wall. "This is not good."

"That must be an old one," she says.

I don't say anything. I can feel the panic circling around me like the fog coming in from the ocean. "This was in Bob's stuff. He probably doesn't take the bus very often," I say in a small voice.

She squints at me the way she did when we first met.

"It's over," I say, even quieter.

Her whole body seems to vibrate with—what? Frustration? Anger? "Do you always give up this easily?"

Now I realize what it is, what's in her voice, her body. Determination.

"Do you, Matilde Gómez?" She says my name like she did that first time, too. Stretched out, slow, like it's foreign and strange. Like it's a bad thing.

But why is she mad at me? This isn't my fault! I stand up. I yank off my backpack and fling it to the ground. "I'm not giving up, Mer-ce-des," I say, stretching out her name the same way she did. "It's called being reasonable. We missed the bus and we have to get home. Why don't you get in touch with reality?"

"Reality? You know what's real? You're scared, Mattie. You're scared of everything. You're scared of taking a stupid book and skipping a field trip. You're scared of doing what you want. You're scared of not doing what people want you to do."

"Right. Because I think about other people, unlike you. I care what my mom thinks and what my friends think. I don't just *do*. I *think*!"

"You *think*? It's called *over*thinking. Why don't you just do something *you* want to do for a change."

"Well, maybe I will!" I scream. "Right now, what I want to do is figure out how to get home. And get away from you!"

"Don't you even care that everyone lied to you? If it weren't for me, you'd never know anything about Frank Gómez. You wouldn't even be here if it weren't for me."

"Exactly!" I shout. "I wouldn't be here if it weren't for you!

I would be at home and I wouldn't have missed the bus and I wouldn't have lied to my mom. I'd be having dinner with my family—you might not know what that is, Mercedes. A family? You know, a bunch of people who love you and want to be with you?"

She looks like she's going to start to cry, but instead she spins around and starts running. Fast. Mercedes's legs move like a graceful racehorse. Her back is straight, her bag flapping against her hip. I wipe at the tears streaming down my face, but I don't look away from her running. Her arms pump at her sides, not taking up extra energy, just moving her forward.

The farther she gets from me, the heavier the rock in my stomach gets. I think of all the people who have left me. Francisco Gómez was the first, even if I never even saw him leave. Our cat, Peacock, who my mom had since she was pregnant with me, died when I was six. Then my grandpa John, my mom's dad, when I was eight. Mai is gone now, too. As I watch Mercedes disappear around the corner of the science building, I know she's right. I *am* scared. I'm terrified of being alone, of being lonely. Of my mom not having time for me. Of my life changing. Of living my new life shared with three strangers. Of being forever the new kid at school. Of being left at Northern Madrone College by myself. Of not finding Francisco Gómez. I scoop up my backpack and run. I don't run gracefully or fast. But I keep my focus and I work hard to catch up with her.

CHAPTER 34

Mercedes

٭

For my twelfth birthday, Mom came home from Brazil and threw me a party. Gaby, Rebecca, Tristan. Emma, Charlotte. Cristina was there. Tristan's dad came, and he and Mom weren't fighting for once. A couple of Mom's friends, Gloria and Anna, who have known me since I was born, came, too. Anyway, there were all these people around the big table in the formal dining room overlooking the ocean. Mom and Gloria were laughing at something Tristan said, and Rebecca and Emily were having a thumb war, and Cristina was showing me how to make my glass sing by running my finger around the edge. Mom let us use her set of fancy crystal goblets, one of the only things she has left from her parents, who both died before I was born.

What I remember most from that night isn't the presents or the world's greatest chocolate cake. What I remember is the sound. Voices talking and laughing, the ringing of the glasses, especially once everyone started making their goblets sing. This, I remember thinking, is the sound of happiness. Of family.

What I hear now is neither of those things. All I hear is the slapping of my sneakers on the sidewalk and the pounding of my heart. Fog is coming in from the ocean in big creeping clouds, and the temperature is dropping. As I get closer to the science building, the only other person I see is a student hurrying toward a dorm beyond the parking lot. It's Friday evening and the campus is emptying out. I'm alone.

Alone except for Mattie. I glance over my shoulder and see that she's running after me. I make a quick right and head toward the student union.

"Wait!" Her voice is ragged.

I shouldn't have turned around again. Because when I do, I see her face. And even though she said mean things to me, I don't want her to be this scared. I slow down. I can hear the sound of that birthday dinner, the sound of family like an echo in my ears. Matilde Gómez is, right now, the closest thing to family I have here in the mountains. We need to stick together. We need a plan.

"We need a plan," Mattie shouts.

I turn around. And go splat on the sidewalk. Sprawling like a baby bird just learning how to fly. One knee and the opposite hand land with a crack.

She rushes forward and helps me up. "You're bleeding." My palm is scraped and dotted with tiny bits of gravel. A splotch of blood drips down my wrist. I pull up the leg of my jeans. More blood on my knee. She digs in her backpack. "Here." She takes a wad of Band-Aids. "D.A.D. supplies come in handy again."

"I hope the Band-Aids work better than your bus schedule," I grumble, but I let her blow on the scrape. I should say thank you. Instead, I say, "You're a really slow runner."

We stare at each other. Is our fight over? Her eyes are wet, but she's not crying anymore.

"Mercedes." She stretches a Band-Aid across my palm. "We need a plan."

"We do," I agree, "what's your plan?"

"I think we sh—"

Whatever her plan is is interrupted by a very loud grumble coming from my stomach. And then, suddenly, like a magic spell, we're both laughing. Coughing and laughing and sputtering.

"If it doesn't involve food, I'm not participating," I say. "Come on, I know where to go."

"Fine," she says, and helps me up.

I think we're going to stick together.

I lead Mattie to the campus cafeteria, where the cross-country team ate after our meet last summer. Today the place is deserted, no one ordering at the counters serving different types of food: pizza, salad bar, soup, sandwich bar, ethnic.

"What's 'ethnic'?" Mattie asks.

"'Stir-fry, enchiladas, gyros,'" I read. Ugh. "Ethnic is just anything that's not burgers and pizza."

"Like us," Mattie says.

"What?"

"You know: we're not just pizza and burgers. We're half Colombian."

I never thought about it like that. "If we're both half Colombian," I say to Mattie, "does that mean that together we make one whole Colombian?"

She grins. "And one whole American?"

"We're already American. We were born here. We live here. We're whole American."

"But then, how can we also be half Colombian? That would make us . . ." Mattie calculates. "One and a half of a person."

"Can I help you?" calls a woman with white hair tucked in a hairnet.

"Um, okay," I say, going over to the grill counter where she smiles at us.

"Hello, you two cutie-pies." The nametag on her white uniform says, *Miss Wiz*.

"Can I get a burger?" Mattie says to Miss Wiz. "Guess I'll be my American half today," she says to me.

"Coming right up, cupcake." Miss Wiz smiles and I see a gold tooth flash in the back of her mouth. "How about you, honey? What I can get you?"

"Do you have vegetarian burgers?"

"We sure do. This is a liberal arts college in California." The woman laughs as loud as a semi. "I'll make you one fresh, sugar." Miss Wiz turns to her grill and makes each of us a burger—gross meat for Mattie and yummy fake stuff for me. She adds a huge pile of fries and a cup of cut-up fruit to each plate. "Now you two sweeties can go up to Linda at the cash register to pay. Tell her the fries are on the house." Miss Wiz winks. "Linda!" she calls, "the fries for these dumplings are on the house!"

"Miss Wiz?" I ask as I take my plate. "Is it always this quiet?"

"Oh, no, honey." Miss Wiz surveys the empty cafeteria. "Friday nights are always slow," she says with a chuckle. "Those kiddos go home, go out to movies, go to the beach."

Mattie and I smile. It's funny to hear college students called "kiddos."

"We're visiting our dad," Mattie volunteers.

I snap my head to look at her. What's the matter with her? She can't tell this cafeteria worker the truth!

"He's working late in the library," she continues. "We didn't have school today so we've been hanging out on campus."

Didn't I tell her to keep it simple? I grab her backpack straps and pull her toward the cashier.

"I thought you didn't like lying," I say once we are seated in a corner of the dining hall.

Mattie shrugs and takes a huge bite of her burger. "It's not a lie. It's a story."

I squirt ketchup on my plate from the bottle at the table. The only reason I like fries is for the ketchup. I dunk in a fry. Delicious.

"What's our plan?" she asks. She eats three fries without any ketchup at all. She's so weird. "I think we should call my mom and go home. She'll be mad, but if we explain everything . . ."

Mom? Go home? I shake my head. "No way. We said no moms."

"Okay, fine. Then we'll call for a ride. Uber or a taxi or whatever. Go to your house."

"No phone, remember?" I hold out my hand and drop an imaginary phone into an invisible pool.

"I'm sure we can find a phone to borrow. We could—"

"But my phone has my money, my Uber account."

"Maybe Miss Wiz has a phone we can borrow?"

I shake my head. "I say we go back to his office and snoop around." I eat four fries with plenty of ketchup and then, with my mouth full, I say, "Maybe we can find out more about him."

"What's the point, Mercedes? He left for the day. And it's Friday, so he's probably not coming back until Monday. Besides, it's night and the whole building is going to be locked."

"But we have to try."

"What are we going to do? Break in?"

"Exactly."

Mattie looks at me like she thinks I've lost my mind. "How?"

"We'll figure it out," I say with more confidence than I feel.

"And then what? How are we getting home?"

"*Then* we'll call your mom and go home."

"That's not much of a plan," Mattie mumbles.

I eat four more fries. They taste best in fours. "Do you have a better one?"

CHAPTER 35

Mattie

'**ve** never been the friend who came up with the good ideas for what to do. Mai always wanted to try new things: a new shop down the block, a park that got a new slide, a new route to school. Sonja has the best imagination and her ideas usually involved putting on theatrical productions or doing elaborate art projects. I've always been the friend who went along with other people's ideas or made sure everyone got a turn. Not everyone has to be the leader. Who would the leaders lead?

So I let Mercedes lead me along the route that's familiar by now—out of the student union, past the Quad, along the field. And then into the trees, where it's dark and—I have to admit—pretty creepy. We run between the yellow spotlights of the lamps that light the sidewalk. We both pretend we're not afraid in the dark spaces in between.

"I'm still not sure about this so-called plan," I say.

"Trust me."

When we reach the Humanities building, she yanks open the door and says triumphantly, "See? Not locked! It's all going to work out."

We haven't seen a single college student since we left the cafeteria, and the Humanities building is just as empty. The lobby feels different in the artificial light of the overhead bulbs. I follow Mercedes back to the anthropology department. No sign of the nosy blue-dress woman. The hallway lights automatically flicker on ahead of us.

Even though we know he's gone and it'll be locked, Mercedes jiggles the doorknob of the office door of the Dupree Visiting Professor.

"Now what?" I ask.

She paces the hallway, tries the other knobs, too. Then she says, "My brother watches this cartoon about a rat and mouse detective. It's super dumb. But they always—"

"Oh, yeah, Lucas watches that one, too. The theme song is so annoying."

"Mattie," Mercedes says, "I'm making a point. Listen. The rat—the girl, of course—is the smart one even though the mouse thinks he's the smart one. Anyway, they figure out how to solve these mysteries by going places that people can't go."

"Right," I say, because I've watched a few episodes with Lucas, pretending not to pay attention. "And then they do that dance at the end when they've solved—"

Mercedes glares at me. I stop talking.

"Well, this is the first floor, right? And if you're thinking like a smart girl-rat, you would figure out that these offices must have windows, right? So all we need to do is go back outside, find the right window and then—"

"Shhhh!" I cup my hand over Mercedes's mouth. "Someone's coming."

We hear whistling. The notes go up and then down, fast and then slow. And then the whistler turns the corner toward the anthropology department hallway and sees us. The whistling stops.

"Hello," says the man in a thick accent. "You surprise me."

"You surprised us!" Mercedes says.

"Can I help you?" The man is wearing gray pants and a shirt that says *Manuel King* on the pocket. He's pushing a cart loaded with a big trash can and cleaning supplies. He has black hair and brown skin and a friendly smile.

"Um, yeah," Mercedes says. She taps the closed office door of Francisco Gómez. "This is our dad's office and we're supposed to meet him here."

I think quick. "He's at the library," I supply.

"He said he left his office unlocked, but I guess . . ."

"I guess he forgot. And our phones are in there. Do you think—"

Mercedes interrupts me. "Do you think you can let us in?"

Manuel King looks around the hallway. "I didn't know Señor Gómez had daughters."

An icy knife goes up and down my spine. We didn't count on him knowing our dad. Will he know that Francisco Gómez doesn't know about his daughters' visit? Does he know Francisco Gómez already left for the day? Will he be suspicious that we're here without him? Is he going to turn us in? Will he call the security guard? Are we about to get arrested?

"You two look just like him," Manuel says with a big smile. "¡Lo mismo! I should have guessed."

I have never felt so relieved in my entire life. Mercedes and I both let out the biggest, longest sighs ever.

Mercedes grins. "That's what everyone says!"

"Are you gemelas?" He seems to expect us to know the Spanish word. We look at him blankly. "Twins?" he translates. We shake our heads. Maybe I should tell him about doppelgängers.

"I have twins. One daughter and one son—a little older than you." Manuel King pulls out a ring of keys. He fits a key in the lock. "They love to visit me at work. I like them to come to Northern Madrone. Maybe someday they'll go to college and won't have to be a custodian like me. They'll be the ones working in the nice offices. Maybe with a hammock like Señor Gómez."

As he says this, Manuel King swings the door open. A hammock is strung across the office. It's striped yellow and blue and red and white and it takes up almost the whole space. You have to duck underneath to get to the desk, which is tucked under the window. I'm so relieved we won't have to break in through that window.

"Does he have a hammock at home, too?" Manuel asks us.

"Yep," says Mercedes.

"Nope," I say—at the same time.

Manuel's smile fades. Why is this the one time we didn't say the same thing?

"I mean, we have one at home *outside*. Not inside like this," Mercedes says quickly. I just nod. I don't trust myself to tell any more stories.

"Ah, well," Manuel King says. He grabs the wastebasket and empties it into his big gray trash can. "If I see Señor Gómez, I tell him his beautiful hijas are here waiting."

"Thanks!" Mercedes says, and then slams the door shut.

My breathing is slowing. "That was close!" I say to Mercedes. "Too close."

"But it worked out," she says. "And now we're in. I told you it was going to be fine." She swings herself into the hammock. "I want one of these in my room." She pushes off a bookshelf, sending the hammock rocking back and forth.

I duck under the hammock and sit in Francisco Gómez's desk chair. This is the chair that my father sits in. There are no blinds on the window and so the glass becomes a mirror. Would he recognize his daughter's face?

The desk is covered in papers and magazines and books. My mom is constantly telling me to clean my room, my desk, my closet. But I always know where everything is. I tell her that putting things away would just make me lose stuff. Francisco Gómez's desk is messier than my room ever is. Maybe he's like me.

"What are you finding?" Mercedes asks.

Just like the search results from Mercedes's phone, the papers and magazines are in Spanish and in English. He's left notes along the margins in green pen. His handwriting is small and neat, mostly capital letters except for the *A*'s. I open the top desk drawer and find a box of green ballpoint pens. "He sure likes green," I say to Mercedes, holding up the box.

"Let's take one," she says. "A souvenir!"

There are probably a dozen pens in the box. "Will he notice if two are missing?"

"He didn't seem to notice two missing daughters."

Her words are like a prick in my finger. I take a pen and toss Mercedes another.

"Keep looking."

I dig deeper. "Just a stack of sticky notes, a bunch of paper clips. That's it," I say, rummaging through the drawer. And in the back, I see a scrap of paper. It's worn and yellowed. Layers of old tape frame the edges. Hand-drawn stars dot the paper. In shaky print, someone has written:

Las estrellas no son la misma cosa para todos. Para los que viajan, las estrellas son guías; para otros solo son pequeñas lúcitas. . . . Pero las estrellas no dicen nada.
—*Antoine de Saint-Exupéry*

I can't read the Spanish words, but I recognize the long name right away. Antoine de Saint-Exupéry. The author of the book on my nightstand at home, *The Little Prince.*

"What else is in there? Any other souvenirs we can take?"

"Nothing." I don't show Mercedes the paper. Or tell her about my book. But I do slip the paper into my pocket.

We dig through the filing cabinet and scan the bookshelves. Mercedes finds a coat hanging on the back of the door and goes through the pockets. There's a rumpled dollar bill that she gives to me. More crime.

"If only Manuel King hadn't emptied the trash," she says. "That's where the mouse and rat always find clues."

"How about these?" I scan the bookshelves. Of course, there are many books with the word "anthropology" in the titles. A stack of magazines is about to slide off the shelf. I straighten it. A book on phylogenetic analysis (whatever that is) rests precariously on the top. I pick it up and something flutters to the floor.

Mercedes drops to her knees. "Photos," she says in a whisper.

We reach for the photos. I turn one over in my hand. It's Francisco Gómez, looking about the same as he does in the picture I have of him. He's standing with a woman whose white hair is cut neatly around her ears. He has his arm around her and her face wrinkles in a smile. They have the same toffee-brown skin and squinty eyes. Eyes like mine. Eyes like Mercedes's.

"I bet that's our grandmother," she says, leaning over my shoulder. I feel that invisible thread connecting us.

A shiver goes up my spine. Our grandmother? My Grandma Barbara went to an assisted living home after Grandpa died. She's forgotten a lot of things, maybe even her own daughter. We didn't see her very often. And now that we moved, I'm not sure when we will again. "I wonder what her name is."

"Look at this one." Mercedes shows me another picture. This one has the same woman looking a little less wrinkled, alongside a man in a white-brimmed hat. She flips the photo over. *"Mami y Papá,"* she reads. *"Matilde Flores and Arturo Gómez."*

We look at each other. "That's my name." I take the photo and flip it over again.

"That's his parents." Mercedes stares at the people who are our grandparents. "I never met Mom's parents. They both died before I was born."

"I thought I was named after Pablo Neruda's wife. The poet. He's a poet that my mom likes."

"Guess you have a family name," Mercedes says, breaking the thread.

My stomach clenches. I know what she's thinking. She's thinking that it's not fair that I got named after our father's mother. And it's not, is it? I don't know what to say. The photo in my hand feels, suddenly, like the reason I'm here in the woods in California. To find this picture. To see this connection. To fill in a bit of the half of me that I didn't realize was missing.

"Wonder who this is." Mercedes has moved on to the other photo in her hand. Francisco Gómez is sitting at a table piled with dishes of food. Next to him is a young woman with long wavy hair. She's wearing glasses, so it's hard to see her eyes, but her nose is a familiar button shape. "A girlfriend?"

I take the photo. "That's got to be another relative. His sister?" I turn over the photo, hoping there's a name on the back. *Francisco y Mechi.*

Mercedes snorts. "What kind of name is Mechi?"

"Mechi," I repeat, tasting the word. Mechi. Mercedes. Mechi. "I bet it's a nickname for Mercedes."

"Yeah, right." Mercedes shakes her head like I've lost it. "I'm named after the wife of Gabriel García Márquez, a Colombian writer. Mom tells me that all the time."

"But you could be named for both. Just like me?" I say as I paw through the other photos. "I bet you're named after his sister." I pick up another picture. "Look, here she is again."

The back of the picture just has the name: *Mechi.* The photo shows the same woman but without the long hair. Her head is wrapped in a pink-and-red scarf and her face is pale and thin.

"This must be the same woman. His sister would be our aunt, Mercedes. Maybe you're named after her."

She shakes her head but then slides both photos of Mechi into her back pocket. "I'm keeping these."

I think of the book, the pen, the piece of paper. What's another theft? "I will, too," I say. I take the photo of Francisco's mom—my grandmother? *Matilde*.

Mercedes climbs back into the hammock. She doesn't look at me or say anything. I sit back down at Francisco's desk and try out the green pen on one of the yellow sticky notes. I write my full name: Matilde Flora Gómez. Then I write Francisco Gómez Flores. The scratching of the pen and the whirring of air-conditioning are the only sounds for a while.

Suddenly Mercedes breaks the silence. "Are you thinking what I'm thinking?" she asks.

"That life is strange?"

"No! That we should stay here tonight." She spreads her arms wide, gesturing to the cramped office of Professor Francisco Gómez. "We said we would stay all night if we had to," she reminds me. "And it looks like we have to."

"What—how? Where?"

"In this office."

"Here?"

"Why not?" Mercedes says, swinging the hammock more. That familiar rock settles in my stomach. I don't know if I can sleep in a cramped office at Northern Madrone College. I don't like not having my own pillow and blanket, having my familiar light beside my bed, the comforting sounds of my mom in the house.

"We both have alibis: your mom thinks you're at my house and Cristina thinks I'm at your house. So let's actually do it."

"Alibis! What is this, a rat and mouse episode?" I shake my head.

"No one will look for us, Mattie. And look!" She grabs the hammock at her sides. "We have a place to sleep!" She holds up a folded wool striped blanket. "And I found this."

"What about pajamas? And toothbrushes?"

Mercedes rolls her eyes at me.

"Where will I sleep?"

"Get in." Mercedes moves over and I climb in so that my feet are near her head. If we balance just right, make enough room for each other, we fit perfectly in the hammock.

CHAPTER 36

Mercedes

☀

want to memorize everything about tonight. I inhale, trying to find my father's scent. I want to learn everything about him. You can find out a lot by watching people and seeing what things they care about. Like Mattie and her Operation D.A.D. supplies—that tells you how much she worries but also how careful and caring she is. There's Tristan's dad with his messy apartment—that shows his energy. Mom and her art and artifacts are proof that she likes to show off—like me, I suppose—and that she likes beautiful things, memorable things. I study Frank's office. What do his things tell me? The jumbled stacks of papers and books say he loves his work. The photos of the women we think are our grandmother and aunt probably mean he loves his family. The funny hammock, woolly blanket, the postcards of Colombia? He loves his country.

And what do my temper tantrums and good grades say about me? What about my matching nail polish? Mattie complimented me on my nails when we went to the bathroom. She wouldn't let us go to bed until we rinsed out our mouths (no toothbrushes) and washed our faces. "It's called Petal Pink," I told her.

"I'm a nail biter, so I never paint my nails." What does it say about Mattie that she destroys her fingernails?

I grabbed her hand and examined her nails. They were short and ragged. "I have a file," I said. "I'll do a manicure on you. I have nail polish in my bag." Her eyes widened. "You're not the only one who can plan ahead," I said, laughing.

At first she protested, but while her nails were drying, she kept holding her hands out, admiring the color and the smoothed-out edges.

"Do you remember Pinocchio?" Mattie asks now from the other end of the hammock.

"Pinocchio?" I repeat, pulling on the blanket again.

A hammock sounds like a comfortable place to sleep, but it's not easy to fit two girls. And each time one of us grabs for more of the blanket, it releases a cloud of dust that makes Mattie sneeze. She's very proud of herself for bringing all her supplies, especially the tissues.

"Pinocchio, you know, the puppet who wanted to be human? With the nose?" Mattie flops and the hammock sways again. "Do you think my nose is growing?"

I've told so many lies. Little lies, like wanting Gaby to come over when I really just wanted to be alone or being fine with sharing my fries with Tristan when I wanted to eat all of them four at a time. And bigger lies like telling Mom that I wanted to have ten girls come to a sleepover at our house, or that I didn't mind that she travels so much.

"Are you sure, Mercedes?" Mom had asked. She was sitting on the edge of my bed like a mom in a movie. Since Tristan was born, she almost never did that anymore. She's the least movie-like mom ever. "I'll be in Australia for eight weeks. It's so far away, there's no point in coming home before the project is done."

"It's fine, Mom," I said, and turned my back to her. I will never tell anyone that I cried that night.

"You take care of Tristan," she had said. But she didn't need to even ask. I will always take care of my brother.

"I hate lying," Mattie says. She's exploring her nose, checking to see if it's growing.

I laugh. "I thought you were enjoying all those stories you made up today."

She giggles, too, but then stops. "I feel terrible for lying to my mom, though. She trusts me. And what if something bad happens? She won't be able to find me."

I push against the wall and make the hammock swing a little like that lullaby. *Rock-a-bye baby in the treetop.* Mom sang that to Tristan when he was a baby. I don't remember if she ever sang it to me.

"It'll be okay." Actually, I have no idea if it'll be okay, but I do know that we can't change any of the choices we made right now. I think of the choice of putting Frank Gómez's picture in my binder. I'm glad I made that choice. "Maybe you need a distraction? Read me something from Professor Gómez's book. The one you stole," I add, and laugh again.

She lets a tiny smile creep into her face. Then she leans out of the hammock and grabs the book from her backpack. The animal shapes on the black cover appear and disappear in the shadows.

"*The Maiden Stars,*" she reads.

"That sounds boring."

"No, listen. It starts in a hammock." Mattie begins to read.

"One night the sun slept peacefully in her hammock. The moon came to her, but she wanted to be left alone so she covered his face in juice, staining it. Later, the sun gave birth to sisters, the Worecu stars. The sisters can always be seen near each other. Some say these stars are Taurus, Jupiter, and Saturn."

"Who are the maidens? Why is the sun in a hammock?" I ask. Mattie shrugs. "Next story!"

"Okay, here's one that says it's an Incan myth. Is that the one in Mexico?"

"You're thinking of the Aztecs. The Inca are in Peru. I thought you studied mythology at your old school."

She ignores me and reads instead.

"Once the maker of everything put a princess in the sky. She had a jug of water, which she poured over the earth. That is how water came to earth. Her brother was put into the sky, too. He was given a club and a catapult, which he sometimes plays with, making thunder and lightning."

"When I was little, I thought thunder was God bowling," Mattie says.

"Tristan says thunder is when the dad from *The Lego Movie* is having a temper tantrum." That's what he said after he watched the movie the first time. He laughed so hard when he was watching the movie that I had my own temper tantrum. Gaby and Rebecca and I were trying to do homework, and I could hear him from upstairs. I yelled at him to stop and I yelled at Cristina to make him stop. I stomped around the living room and threw one of Mom's vases from Japan on the floor. Talk about thunder. Gaby and Rebecca went home early that day. Not that I'm going to tell Mattie any of this.

"You must get along with your brother," Mattie says.

"He's a pain," I answer. But that's not the whole answer. He *is* a pain, but he's *my* pain. "What about your stepbrothers?"

"I hardly know them," Mattie says. "I mean, sometimes it seems like it could be kind of cool. Like, I sometimes play chess with the ten-year-old. I went on a ride with my little stepbrother at the Boardwalk and that was pretty fun. Until he puked on me."

I feel a guilty thump in my stomach. I don't tell her that I saw it happen, that my friends were laughing at her.

"I mostly don't talk to them. I mean, even when Kenny and I play chess, we don't talk. I don't know what to say. What do you say to your brother?"

"I don't know. Normal stuff." I never thought about what I say to Tristan. I suppose it would be weird to suddenly have a new family. "I ask him about first grade and his friends. I tell him about stuff I did when I was his age."

"I don't know if they want to hear about what I did when I was their age. They tiptoe around me like I'm an explosive."

"Are you?" I ask. Something in my chest flutters. Maybe I'm not the only one who has temper tantrums.

"Me? Never," she says.

My heart closes. "Let's just go to sleep, okay?" I reach as far as I can and flip the light switch. The hammock sways wildly back as Francisco Gómez's office—and Mattie—disappears into darkness.

CHAPTER 37

Mattie

The noise is like a mouse scritch-scratching. In my dream, a mouse and rat hold a tiny copy of *The Seed Sower* and gnaw on the beautiful black cover. My eyes snap open. Where am I? I tear off the stinky, dusty blanket. It's a very early gray, dim morning. In Francisco Gómez's office. And everything comes rushing back. The stolen book, the skipped field trip, the poem, the lies. I sneeze, sending the hammock swinging. This causes Mercedes to kick me in the ribs. I shove her back. I open my mouth to holler at her.

At the same time, the scritch-scratching noise becomes the sound of a key turning in a lock. There's a click. The door of Francisco Gómez's office swings open. And there, in the doorway, is a man who must be our father.

Except he clearly doesn't know he's our father. His eyes widen as he looks from the hammock to his desk, from our bags and shoes on the floor to our faces. Now we're flailing in the hammock, each of us trying to get out, which makes the hammock twist and turn. Mercedes is trying to grab onto the wall to stabilize herself, but that just sends me tipping further.

"What—" he begins.

Mercedes crashes to the floor.

"—is—"

I tip the other direction, landing with a thud, the blanket tumbling over my head.

"—this?"

I can hear Mercedes scuffling to her feet as I grab at the blanket. I sneeze again.

"¡Juepucha! ¿Quiubo, nenas? ¿Qué te me hagan?" Francisco Gómez is sputtering in Spanish.

We scramble to our feet. Me and Mercedes. Rumpled from head to toe, and our hair—even hers—has gone wild, sticking up in every direction. My sister and I stand side by side in front of our father.

For a long time, none of us moves. The only sound is me sniffling—I may sneeze again. He stares at us, the key still in the lock, his hand on the door frame. We must have startled him. He looks back and forth between the two of us. He's probably wondering if we're thieves or burglars or runaways. We're all that and more, of course. Does he recognize us? We look exactly alike right now—our brown eyes big, our mouths waiting to see if we should frown or smile. Our hair, wavy and wild. Our matching Petal Pink fingernails. Does he know we're his daughters? The longer the silence goes, the faster my heart beats. Will he yell at us? My head is filled with rocks. Will he throw us out, call the security guard? Am I going to jail? Black spots appear in front of my eyes. Will I faint?

Mercedes takes my hand and squeezes, just for a moment. I take a deep, brave breath. "Francisco Gómez," I say in a clear, calm voice.

"Hi, Frank," Mercedes says.

There were many things I imagined he might do when he saw us. I imagined he'd be angry. I imagined he'd be happy. I imagined that he'd ask about our moms, ask us how old we are, ask us how we got here. I imagined he might want proof (would my school ID work? My baby picture?). What I didn't imagine is that he would fall to his knees in front of us and start crying.

It doesn't take much for me to cry. My mom says I cried at the smallest noise when I was a baby. When I was a toddler, I sobbed every day when she dropped me off at day care. I cried on my first day of kindergarten and on my last day of sixth grade. I still cry—a bad grade, a broken pencil, a look from a teacher. I cry when I'm worried that I'm going to have a panic attack, and I also cry when I see a cute puppy at the park.

My mom cries a lot, too. She always cried on Christmas morning when it was just the two of us and she opened whatever present I made her—a lopsided bowl, a ragged pot holder. She cries at the end of sad movies and blows her nose really loudly. She used to cry at work because she hated her job. She cries when I sing "Over the Rainbow" to her.

But this kind of crying isn't like any of that crying. The sound coming from Francisco Gómez isn't sad and it's not sobbing like a baby. But it's also not tender like crying over music or puppies. The sound of his crying is something different. Something beyond sad or scared or hurt or angry. Francisco Gómez reaches out for us and before I know it, my father has his arms around both me and Mercedes. We're a cluster of stars. All of us, together.

CHAPTER 38

Mercedes

The three of us are cramped in the small space of floor between the office door and the hammock. And I think, *Now what?* I didn't think this far when I imagined looking for him. I glance at Mattie. I can tell by her face that she didn't, either.

"Daughters of mine. Mis hijas," Frank Gómez says. I was starting to wonder if he would ever let go of us and if he would ever stop crying.

"You know who we are?" Mattie asks.

He nods, wipes his face with his shirt.

"Of course." He swallows. A few more tears drip down his face. I certainly did not imagine all the crying. "Look." He shifts and reaches into his jacket pocket. He pulls out a worn leather wallet. The pocket for dollar bills is stuffed with little scraps of paper. He digs through the papers—sticky notes and receipts and ticket stubs—and pulls out two worn squares. Photos.

The first one is the same baby picture Mattie brought with her. I take this copy from his hands and flip it over. *Querido Francisco – Our beautiful daughter. Matilde, just like you wanted.*

"Which one?" he asks, looking back and forth between us.

Mattie snatches it from me. "That's me."

I wait for the second one. He holds it out. Me. My baby picture. I'm wearing a ridiculous pink dress with ruffled pink pants that cover my diapers. I'm chubby and—I have to admit—really cute. I flip it over. Mine just has my name and birthdate written in Mom's block print. Nothing more. I hand it back to him. It's obvious, I suppose, that the second photo is me. That I'm Mercedes.

He wipes his eyes with the back of his hand and grins. "It's a such a surprise. Like Christmas. Or New Year's. A big surprise. But one I feel like I've been waiting for my whole life. You two—you're like two ghosts. Ghosts of your mothers. Ghosts of . . ." He pauses. "Ghosts of myself."

I can't decide if I'm a little freaked out right now or if this is cool. My foot starts tapping nervously on the tile floor of his office. Is this what I wanted?

"Tell me everything," he says. Mattie returns the picture, and he tucks them both back into his wallet. Then he takes our hands—one in each of his large, brown ones. The hand that is holding mine has a scar across the back that looks like a burn. Was it from a fire under the Amazon skies? The pressure of his grip is strangely comforting.

"How did you get here? Are you well? How do you know each other? What are you doing here? How did you find me? How are you? Do you need breakfast?"

When he talks, each of his words is short, like he can't wait to get to the next one. The *H*'s are harsh and strange. He doesn't sound as much like Ruben Hernandez as I thought he would. Frank Gómez has more wrinkles around his eyes than he did when the photo I have was taken. But even with the lines, the eyes are as familiar as my own. Or Mattie's. His hair is curly, almost puffy. He needs a trim. Around the ears, he has bits of gray. But not as much as Mom does when she's overdue for a trip to her salon.

"Now," he says, "Matilde." He looks at Mattie, saying her name with a lilt. "You are, what? Thirteen?"

A red glow seeps into her face. "Next month." She's smiling.

He turns to me. "And Mercedes." He gently rolls the *R* in my name and the *C* is soft. "Let me see. You're twelve. Do I have that right?" He smiles. "Where are you mothers? Where is Valeria? Where is Jennifer?" He looks around the little office as if our moms are hiding in the filing cabinet. "I would love to see them. You each look like your mother. They were beautiful, both of them. Like you. You are both beautiful." His voice catches like a snag in a sweater. "Are you really here? Matilde? Mercedes? Mis hijas perdidas."

I don't know what his Spanish words mean, but they make my heart sad. My whole body feels heavy with sadness, and I'm not sure why. I imagined that meeting Frank Gómez would be exciting. Thrilling. Not sad. I feel a rush of heat thrumming through my body. I'd rather feel angry than sad. I clench my fists. But then the large brown hand on mine squeezes even harder. I loosen my fingers. The angry feeling seeps into the cold floor.

Frank Gómez sniffs. He clears his throat. "How did you get here? Girls your age cannot be at the college without parents, can they?" He looks from me to Mattie and back to me again. Can he tell running away was my idea?

"We—"

"I—"

Me and Mattie in unison. Again.

Only this time, I'm glad.

"Our moms aren't here, actually," she says. "It's just us."

"We wanted to meet you," I add.

And we tell this man, this stranger, this Frank Gómez, the story about meeting each other, about our day and our night and about how we didn't plan the ending. We don't tell any lies. Only the truth. We tell as many truths as we can. Frank Gómez just nods as we talk. He doesn't get off the floor and he doesn't let go of our hands.

"And now," Mattie says, a quiver in her voice, "we don't know what happens next."

We'll be fine, I mouth.

Then she asks in a small voice, "Are you mad at us?"

The whole time we've been sitting here, I've been hoping that Frank Gómez isn't mad at us. I know what mad is. I know what it feels like to be angry at someone, at no one, at everyone.

"Of course not. How can I be angry?" He scoops us into another group hug. "Mis niñas." He shakes his head. He smiles. Then his brow wrinkles. "But," he says, "it looks like we need to figure out what happens now. The rest of the story."

"How will we get home?" Mattie asks.

Then he smiles again. "I have an idea."

"You do?"

For once, I'm glad I'm not in charge. Usually, I love being in charge. I love telling people what to do. Another reason why Mom thinks I'll make a great CEO of a big company. I feel a rush of relief that I don't have to decide what to do now. It's not up to me to figure out what happens next.

"Breakfast," he says with a wink. "I haven't had my coffee yet. Let's go to the cafeteria."

It's the least parent-like thing he could say. It sounds like something I would say. I smile.

He stands up and brushes off the seat of his pants. Mattie and I do, too, and we pull on our sneakers and sweatshirts. Mattie hands me a hair tie and we both pull our hair into ponytails. While we're getting organized, Frank Gómez gathers a pile of papers from his messy desk and stuffs them in a bag. He pulls a book from his shelf and puts that in, too.

"Got everything?" he asks, his hand on the doorknob, ready to leave his office.

We look around the room. Our little home for one night. I run my fingers along the cotton of the hammock. Mattie does the same at the other end. And then she says, "Um, we took this from the library."

She pulls *The Seed Sower* from its nest in the hammock.

"Ah, my book!" he says, and takes it from her. "Patricia works fast. I didn't think she would have it processed and ready for checkout yet."

"No," Mattie says. "We didn't check it out—we stole it. We're sorry."

And then Frank Gómez lets out the biggest, most beautiful guffaw I've ever heard. The tension in my hands eases. Mattie's face relaxes. His laughter fills his messy office, bounces off the filing cabinet, surfs over the hammock, circles the desk, brushes past the bookshelves, and lands back in my ears.

CHAPTER 39

Mattie

⚙

You found your dad!" Miss Wiz says in a big voice when we get to the cafeteria. She doesn't know how right she is. A student wearing penguin pajamas is at the waffle bar. She doesn't look up. "Professor Gómez," Miss Wiz calls, "I didn't realize these two were your girls."

Francisco Gómez grins. "This is Matilde, and this is Mercedes."

I love the way he says our names, even as he's pushing us toward the waffles. *Matilde.* My mom started calling me Mattie when I was learning how to talk. It was easier for me to say, she told me. She has a video of me saying, "My name is Mattie," in a squeaky voice. I never liked the name Matilde, but the way my father says, "Matilde," it sounds soft and joyful, not at all weird or different.

We pick and choose our breakfasts (waffles with whipped cream and strawberries for me, syrup and butter for Mercedes, scrambled eggs from Miss Wiz for our dad). We sit at a small round table near the windows that face the Quad. Beyond the library, the fog is escaping the woods, making the green of the trees extra brilliant. The campus is quiet now, no evidence of the protest or juggler from yesterday. The only proof that yesterday even happened is us here with our father.

"Much better," Francisco Gómez says after taking a long gulp of coffee. "I came to work even before I had my coffee. I need to finish this application today and I forgot all the paperwork in my office." He pats his messenger bag, where he stashed *The Seed Sower*. I miss the weight of it in my backpack. "Lucky for us that I did. Qué suerte."

"What application?" Mercedes asks, her mouth full of waffle.

"I'm applying for a grant."

"What for?"

"You see, I'm an anthropologist. *Etnografía*. How do you say it? An ethnographer. I study groups of people, different native cultures in South America. For many years, I've worked with the Arhuaco people in Colombia. I need funding— money—to return to the Sierra Nevada de Santa Marta to continue my work."

Returning to Colombia? Does he notice that Mercedes's face has turned white, two splotches of red on each cheek? I glance under the table and see her fists. He doesn't look at either of us but rummages around in his bag. Is he looking for *The Seed Sower*? No. He takes out a big, bulky phone, not a brand that I've seen before.

"Look, here is a family of Arhuaco. This is the mother and her three children, all girls." Francisco Gómez hands us the phone and we see a picture of a brown-skinned woman with black hair and a white dress. The three girls next to her wear the same white clothes and carry woven bags on their shoulders. They're smiling at the camera. A cluster of stars.

"Arhuacos have mostly remained separate from modern

society. They live on the same land they've lived on for centuries. But climate change is having a very bad impact on them—their land, their way of life."

I'm suddenly glad we went to the protest yesterday.

"It's important for their culture to be understood, protected, respected. This woman's grandfather is one of the leaders. He's called a *mamu*. He's a great storyteller. I'm learning so many stories from them. Stories that I hope will help people understand."

Our father stares at the image on the screen like it holds secrets. Like the picture itself is going to start telling him a story. I want him to look at us. We have stories, I want to tell him.

"You're not staying in California?" Mercedes has a drip of syrup on her chin. Her fork drops with a clatter.

"I'm only here at Northern Madrone until December."

"But—" I want to say something, but I don't know what it should be. Is there something I can say to keep him here? Instead, I blurt, "Do you have a wife? Children? I mean, other children?"

Our father shakes his head. "I never married again. I never had more children." Then he taps his phone. "But these people, the people I study, are like family. The other humans you spend your time with—it doesn't matter if you're related to them or not. They start to feel like family. Like home."

I think about the people in my house. Bob and Lucas and Kenny. When will they feel like family? Like home?

"What about us?" Mercedes asks. Her words jab through her clenched teeth.

Francisco Gómez doesn't say anything at first. He tucks the phone back in his bag. He doesn't look at us.

"Yeah," I say in a small voice, "what about us?"

He sighs. His hair on his forehead flutters in the rush of air. He takes another sip of coffee.

"This is very hard for me to talk about. I have always wondered what I would tell you, mis hijas, if I ever had the chance to meet you." Mercedes and I don't take our eyes off him. "I thought I wanted a life with your mother, Matilde. When I met Valerie, I thought that we would be happy, that a life in Minnesota was all I would need. We were in love. She was so happy. But I wasn't happy. I realized that I needed to be back in Colombia. In the field. The mountains. The jungle. To do my work, to be myself. I didn't know how to be myself in Minnesota. So I let her go."

He let me go, too, I think.

"And what about *my* mom?" Mercedes demands. Tears are leaking out of the corner of her eyes.

"Jennifer was such an adventurer. So strong. Is she still like that? She went into the mountains with me for a couple weeks— did she tell you? But I had to stay, and she had to leave. She didn't tell me until later about the baby that would come. You."

"Didn't you ever want to meet us?"

Francisco Gómez studies his hands, folded on the tabletop. It's like he's trying to decide what to say, which words to use. But he wrote a whole book, so shouldn't he know all the words?

"Your mother, Matilde, and your mother, Mercedes," he says at last, "they wanted to protect you from missing a man who spends all of his time in the jungle."

The way he says the word "jungle" makes it sound like a different planet, a faraway solar system. He says "jungle" like it means more than trees and animals, like it's a place where no one can follow him. Is the jungle a place with many secrets, just like the sky in his poem?

"They both wanted it this way. And I needed to respect what they wanted. Valerie, Jennifer. They are the mothers. They decide what is best."

My mom told me he didn't want to come back to Minnesota. Mercedes's mom told her they were better off without him. They both told us he didn't have time for children. But those things weren't the whole truth. He looks up. His eyes are wet, and I feel an ache deep in my heart. It sinks, heavy. And I can tell that the things he never said—the letters he never sent, the emails he never wrote, the poem he never shared—that wasn't the whole truth, either. I can see in his eyes that he wanted to see us, to know us. If you only tell half the story, is that the same as a lie? My mom and Mercedes's mom told us what they thought was best, but is it ever best to tell only part of the story?

"We should go." He smiles a little sadly and stands up. As if that's the end. He slings his bag over his shoulder and stacks our dishes on a tray.

"But it doesn't have to be like that," I protest. We follow him as he puts the tray on the conveyor belt that carries the dirty dishes away, out of sight. "You're here now. We can get to know you." I point at Mercedes. "I mean, Mercedes and I just met. And now we're, like, sisters."

"Well, half sisters," Mercedes clarifies.

"Sisters," Francisco Gómez repeats. "Hermanas. Do you know that's how you say 'sisters' in Spanish?"

"Err-mah-nahs," we repeat. In unison.

"Buen hecho," he says. "Good job."

We walk outside. The sun is beginning to peek through the fog. On the steps of the student union, he puts an arm around each of us.

"Ay, mis estrellitas," he says.

And somehow I know right then that we'll never know everything. That some things will stay a mystery. Mercedes and I lock eyes as he squeezes us. We walk awkwardly, the three of us like an unsteady creature trying to find its way.

In the parking lot, Francisco Gómez opens the passenger door of his little green car. He's going to drive us home to Santa Cruz. First to my house. I'm not sure what we will tell my mom, what story we'll give her.

There's only one seat in front and there are two of us, so Mercedes and I decide to sit in the back seat together. "I feel like a taxi driver!" he says, laughing. He starts the car and opens his window. He inhales deeply. "I love the smell of the woods here in California. It reminds me of the mountains outside Quito, Ecuador." He rolls out of the parking lot, turning the same direction as the protesters had gone.

"So, daughters of mine," Francisco Gómez says once we're heading south toward Santa Cruz. "Did you read my book— *The Seed Sower*?" He looks away from the road for a split second and pats the messenger bag on the seat beside him.

"You mean the one Mattie stole?" Mercedes says. He chuckles.

A punch of guilt hits my gut. "We read, um, some of it."

He laughs his big guffaw again, filling his small car with

the booming sound. "Well, I want to tell you a story from the book. From the Arhuaco people. Once upon a time," he begins, "in dark times, before there was light, an Arhuaco woman gave birth to two children. Hermanos. Siblings, like you two. Twins."

Maybe they were doppelgängers.

"These children glowed, a brilliant light shining from them. They were beautiful. Afraid that the people of her village would want to kidnap her children because of their beauty, the woman hid her children in a cave, covering the entrance with large stones. But through the cracks, the people of the village saw the light shining. It was so beautiful, they wanted to see what made this light. La luz. Do you know what *la luz* is?"

We both shake our heads.

"Light," our father says. "*La luz* means 'light.' Did you know that in Spanish, when a mother gives birth to a baby, we say that she gave light? Dar luz."

I watch the sun sparkle on the blue ocean as we speed toward home. Far off on the horizon, fog fights with the sun. "*Luz*," I repeat softly. The word feels happy and safe in my mouth.

"Well," our father continues, "the villagers came to the cave one night. They brought instruments and played music. The music was so beautiful that the brother, Yuí, couldn't help but come out to hear it. As soon as the people saw Yuí, they tried to grab him. But he flew into the sky where he became the sun. The next night, the people returned to the cave and saw that light still glowed. Again they played beautiful music until the sister, Tima, emerged. She was so lovely. The villagers didn't want her to get away, so they threw ashes in her face, hoping to stop her. But Tima flew into the sky in the same direction as her brother. Her face was covered in ashes, so she wasn't as bright as the sun."

"The moon," Mercedes says, interrupting the story.

"Very good, Mercedes," our dad says. The way he says it makes me wish I had guessed. "She became the moon. And at night she watches over the Arhuacos. And that's very comforting."

"So this Tima is just like Selene. In Greek mythology. Only a different story," Mercedes says with a snort. "It's all just stories."

CHAPTER 40

Mercedes

B y the time Frank finishes his stupid story about the sun and the moon, I'm boiling. The sun streams in the car window. I'm sure my left arm is getting sunburned. My shoulders ache from spending the night in the hammock. The seat belt in this tiny car cuts into my neck.

Meanwhile, Mattie is gazing at Frank Gómez like he has all the answers.

Mattie. With her family. Her mom. A stepdad. Step-brothers. All watching over her like the moon watching those Colombian people. Who is watching over me? Mom—she's in Japan. Cristina's paid to do it. Tristan? He's just a seven-year-old. It's *my* job to watch over *him*.

"Where do you live?" Mattie is asking. "Can we see your house? Can we visit you?"

Frank smiles, shakes his head. "I live near Northern Madrone College, in a house for college guests. I don't know if you can visit. We need to talk to your mothers. They will decide. One thing at a time, Matilde."

"My mom never told me anything about you," Mattie says.

Frank just nods.

"Neither did mine," I offer.

He nods again.

"Once upon a time," he begins.

Great. Another story.

"Once upon a time there was a man. He loved adventure and learning. He traveled all around the world to the highest mountains and the lowest valleys. He met new people and heard fantastic stories. He traveled to warm blue seas and cold rivers. He saw many things, but he was always alone."

I slouch in my seat. I cross my arms over my chest. I don't want to hear another story from Frank Gómez. I don't want to hear about what happened; I want to know what's *going* to happen.

"He traveled alone, and he often traveled at night. Because, at night, he didn't feel so lonely. Even in the dark, you can see things. He saw the moon smiling down at him. He saw the stars winking at him. And he knew he was never alone."

I don't realize that the story is over until Mattie asks, "Is that—" she begins. "Is that a story from the people you study in Colombia?"

The car hums on the road.

"No, my dear," Frank Gómez says. "That is a true story. It is my story."

"You're the man?" I ask. "But you're an adult. You don't have to be alone. Not if you don't want to be."

Frank switches on his turn signal and checks his mirrors. He pulls over at a gravel clearing on the side of the road overlooking the ocean. He gets out of the car and Mattie and I follow.

"Look at this view," he says, gazing out across the water.

Mattie and I stand beside him. She looks obediently. I try to not look, but the ocean sparkles like it's desperate for my attention. The water below is blue, crashes in foamy waves on the rocks. It's the kind of view Mom loves. In fact, I'm pretty sure I've been to this very overlook before.

"Look," he says, pointing up the coast. "North, right?"

We squint in the sun. The waves pound out a rhythm.

"North, south, east, west." I want to roll my eyes. Where is this going?

"You know the directions," he says, almost like he's proud of me.

I'm in seventh grade, I want to say, *of course I know the directions.*

"The sun sets in the west and rises in the east, right? Straight above at noon?" He squints at the sun. "Right now, it's almost noon, isn't it?"

We nod. Duh.

"So people know which way is which. The sky helps people navigate. In the day, the sun. And at night, the stars. People still use the stars to tell them things. To show the way."

My foot taps on the dirt. I remember the students Aiden and Kelly discussing Professor Gómez's lecture. Is he going to lecture us like he does his college students?

"Do you know what a compass is?"

"Of course," I say. I feel jittery. This time I do roll my eyes.

"It's another thing we use to tell which direction we're going. Right? The magnetic needle of a compass always points north no matter how you turn it." Frank leans against the low wooden railing between the parking lot and the cliff. The railing is too short to actually keep anyone out. I suppose it's more like a rule—it can be broken if you want to bad enough. "Everyone has a compass inside them. Only, instead of pointing north, it points to what they're meant to be, what they're supposed to do. And no matter what you do, you cannot change that magnetic needle."

"Are you saying that you have a compass?" I ask. I'm starting to understand why he's giving us this lecture. And it has nothing to do with college.

He nods.

"Your compass points to Colombia?"

He nods again.

"And your work? You need to do your work, no matter what?"

"Exactly." He looks sad. "We can't help which direction our compass needle points. Sometimes, we have to just follow it. For me, that means working in Colombia."

Mattie's face scrunches. "Does a compass tell you where you belong?"

"No one and nothing can tell you where you belong, Matilde," Frank says. "You get to choose. But the compass helps you figure out what's important."

"I don't think I have a compass."

"If you pay attention, you'll notice it."

"My mom must not have a compass, either," she says. "She was glad when she lost her job. So her work must not be that important to her."

"Or maybe her compass points to her family. To you," Frank says.

"*My* mom works no matter what. She runs her company. She travels. She's never home," I say as we look out over the water. Across the ocean is Japan—and Mom. "Maybe, I guess, because of her compass?"

He nods again. "Sometimes the pull from this compass takes us away from the people we love." He puts an arm around each of us and pulls us in.

I feel my shoulders loosen from the weight of his arms. And also, maybe, from his words. "A compass tells you where you're going, right?" I say in a small voice.

Our father squeezes me tighter. "A compass points you in the right direction."

CHAPTER 41

Mattie

The closer we get to my house, the more my stomach ties itself in knots, as tightly woven as the rope of the hammock. Mercedes helps me give Francisco Gómez directions. As he turns onto the street where Bob's house is, my hands go cold and sweaty. I wipe them on my jeans and ball my fists so I can't see the bubblegum-pink nail polish on my fingers. He pulls the Prius into the driveway. I squeeze my eyes shut. I see stars blinking so I open them again. All the choices we made over the last twenty-four hours stack up on my shoulders. What will my mom say? How much trouble will I be in? What will happen when she sees Francisco Gómez?

The three of us are silent in the car. No one moves. Mercedes doesn't look at me, just stares out the window. I can see her forehead wrinkle like she's trying to solve an impossible math problem.

And then the bright-red front door opens. My mom comes out in shorts and a sweatshirt. She walks barefoot on the brick sidewalk to the driveway. She waves, she squints, shielding her eyes from the sun. I scramble out of Francisco Gómez's car. I run to her and bury my face in her shoulder. Her hair smells freshly washed with the same shampoo she's always used. The scent reminds me of my old home, of Saint Paul, of Minnesota, of cold autumns and snowy winters. Of all the nights and days of just me and her. My mom and me together. The two of us. It smells like home. And I realize this is home. Wherever she is.

"What's the matter, Mattie-mouse?" She strokes my hair. "How was the sleepover? Did something happen at your friend's house? Why are you crying? Are you okay?"

And then I hear the car door opening. The gritty footsteps of a man's shoes on concrete. Through her sweatshirt, I feel my mom's heart skip for a split second.

"What—" she says with a gasp.

I step away from my mom and the whole world seems to stop. I can't believe I'm seeing my mom and my dad together. My mom's mouth is open like she's about to speak. Or shout. Or laugh. Francisco Gómez's eyes avoid hers. But he's smiling shyly. I wonder what it was like when they first met. They were both in college. College students like the ones at Northern Madrone. Did they stare at each other like this?

"Valerie," my dad says. His accent makes the *V* sound like a *B*. Like my mom is someone else.

"Francisco?"

"I've brought your daughter."

Your daughter, my father says to my mother. Not *our* daughter.

"How—" my mom begins.

But then the other car door opens and Mercedes steps out.

My mom looks back and forth between me and Mercedes. "Who—" she tries again.

"This is Mercedes," our father says. "Mercedes Miller."

My mom looks at me, stunned. "*This* is your new friend? *This* is Mercedes?" She turns to Francisco. "Is she—"

"Mercedes is my daughter."

"They look like—" my mom begins. "They look like twins."

"Yes, they are very close in age."

There's a long silence.

"The divorce was a long time ago, Francisco," my mom says. And then she repeats Mercedes's name like everything makes sense now. "I should have guessed. And she must be named after—"

"Yes." Francisco Gómez bows his head.

"I'm named after the wife of Gabriel García Márquez," Mercedes volunteers.

"Yes, of course," my mom says, her voice full of wonder. "It's a beautiful name." She moves toward Mercedes as if she's going to hug her. I don't think that's a good idea.

"Mercedes Barcha, yes. But you're named after my sister, too," our father says. "Mercedes Gómez Flores. It was all I asked of your mother."

My mom asks, "How is Mechi?"

Mechi? I sneak a look at Mercedes. I was right.

Our dad shakes his head sadly and tells my mom, "She didn't make it."

"I'm so sorry. Your sister was a wonderful person." My mom squeezes me again. "This is why we give our children family names. To remember."

"Just like Matilde," our father says. "Named for my mother." I smile. "Matilde and Mercedes. Family names."

"And also literary names," my mom says. We are both

named after wives of famous writers and also given family names. Sometimes two things can be true at the same time.

"Mattie and Mercedes."

"Yes," says Francisco Gómez. "Names have stories."

"And now, you two." My mom looks back and forth between me and Mercedes. "I'd like to hear your story."

CHAPTER 42

Mercedes

✻

Mattie's mom invites us all into the house. The house is small, a lot smaller than mine. Weavings hang on the bright-yellow walls and a large painting above the TV of a mountain landscape reminds me of the photo of Francisco Gómez. Each piece of furniture is a different color, and all flat surfaces are crowded with trinkets—little ceramic cars, painted leopards, stacks of books. My own house is all shades of white and gray—all very minimal. Mom says that when you face the ocean, you don't want any color to distract. Our house is made to show off to visitors, but Mattie's house feels like it's meant for the people who live in it.

In the living room, I choose a dark-red-striped chair. Mattie sits on the turquoise sofa next to her mom. Frank Gómez perches on the edge of a wooden rocking chair. He looks unsteady.

Mostly Mattie does the talking. Frank cuts in sometimes. He apologizes over and over. Sometimes in English, sometimes in Spanish. Mattie's mom keeps her arm around Mattie the whole time, like she's afraid she'll disappear again. She speaks in a stern, teacher-like voice to Mattie about lying to her. About how anything could have happened. About how we could have been in real danger at Northern Madrone College all by ourselves. And then she kisses the top of Mattie's head. "I'm so glad you're all right."

"Hello." A tall, thin man in blue basketball shorts walks into the living room. He looks at Frank and at me. And then at Mattie and her mom. "What's going on here?"

"This is Bob," Mattie's mom says. "My husband." She smiles at him like he invented the sun and the stars. It's disgusting to see old people in love. "Bob, this is Mattie's father, Francisco, and this is . . ." She pauses.

I glare at her. What is she going to say? How will she explain me to her husband? Who am I?

"This is Francisco's other daughter." I listen for her to stop there. To not explain anything. But then she adds, "Mattie's half sister."

A tingle courses through me from my toes to my cheeks.

So now they explain everything all over again. This time Frank speaks more. He keeps saying he had no idea that we all lived so close. He had no idea that Mattie and her mom were living in California. He thought me and Mom were still in San Francisco and he didn't know how close the city is to Northern Madrone College. And even if he did, he never would have imagined that the girls would try to find him. He's so sorry. Mattie's mom is more relaxed now, offers the adults coffee. She tells Mattie to take me in the kitchen to get zucchini bread. I can tell she's trying to get rid of us.

"Is this weird or what?" I say when we're in the little red-and-white kitchen.

"Do you want zucchini bread?" Mattie asks.

"What is it? It sounds gross." She's still so weird.

"It's good." Mattie shrugs. "It's a Minnesota thing, I guess." She slices two thick pieces of bread and we sit at the small kitchen table that overlooks the backyard. A soccer ball and a green bike are on the grass. Not much different from the things Tristan leaves in our backyard. Brothers, stepbrothers. Maybe not that different from sisters or half sisters.

"Now what? Are you going to be grounded?" I take a bite of zucchini bread and realize I'm starving. The waffles we ate at Northern Madrone's cafeteria seem like ages ago.

"I don't know. I've never been grounded."

This doesn't surprise me.

She chews. "Of course, I've never run away before, either."

We look at each. We can't help bursting into giggles.

We're still laughing when a whirlwind swirls into the kitchen: a blond boy about Tristan's age and a taller, skinnier boy are arguing over something having to do with balls or goals. They don't seem to notice Mattie at first. But when they do, they get quiet.

"Hi," the older one says. He's shy, like he's scared of her. I can't imagine anyone being scared of Mattie.

"This is Mercedes," Mattie says, "She's my half sister."

For a moment the words "half sister" hang in the kitchen.

"This is Kenny. The chess master." The older boy turns red. "And this is Lucas."

"Cool!" Lucas shouts.

"My brother, Tristan, is about your age," I tell him.

"Cool!" he says again.

I can tell they like her; they're just shy. Then Lucas and Kenny grab slices of zucchini bread with dirty hands. Gross.

"Your stepbrothers adore you," I say after the two boys take off into the backyard.

She looks at me like I'm crazy. "They act like I don't exist."

"I know little boys," I assure her. "They like you. Just give them time."

When Mattie's mom calls to us a few minutes later, we return to the living room, where she tells us, "First, we need to contact your mom. She must be terribly worried, Mercedes."

Right. Mom doesn't even know where I am. "She's out of town for work," I say. "I have a nanny. If someone can give me a ride home, I'll be fine."

But this doesn't work with the grown-ups.

"Well, then, your nanny will be worried about you," Mattie's mom says.

I roll my eyes. Cristina thinks I'm at Mattie's house. Which is true. I'm here now, aren't I? "My nanny won't even realize."

Still, they insist on calling both Cristina and Mom. Something about Frank being there, something about responsibility and "it's only right." I reluctantly give them the numbers. First they call Cristina and tell her that they'll drop me off later. Then they call Mom. No answer. It's much later—or is it earlier?—in Tokyo. She's probably sleeping or having dinner with clients or hunched over her laptop in some hotel room. Mattie's mom leaves a message about urgently wanting to talk to Mom about me. She says that she's my friend's mom. I notice that she *doesn't* say that she's my dad's ex-wife.

"We'll try calling her again in a little while. Why don't you all stay for lunch?" Mattie's mom says. "Bob, maybe you could grill a couple hot dogs?"

"I don't eat meat."

"No problem, Mercedes," Mattie's mom says with a smile. "We have some vegetarian hot dogs. And salad."

Bob leaps into action; Frank stands. The adults politely help one another. The clatter of dishes and the mumbled voices make my toes curl. I flash back to that birthday dinner. The sound of family. Togetherness. Then my mind flashes to Mattie: *You don't even know what a family is.*

I glare at the whole commotion. I have to get out of here. I slip away and burst into the blinding afternoon sun. Even from here, I can hear those sounds. The sound of family. I just want to get away. Far away. Away from my half sister. Away from Frank Gómez. Why did I ever think that finding him would change anything? I glance back at the obnoxiously cheery red door of Mattie's house. I start running.

CHAPTER 43

Mattie

Watching Francisco in the kitchen with my mom and Bob is like watching Buzz Lightyear with Cookie Monster. They're from different worlds. Different sets of rules. My father, Francisco, is polite: offering, apologizing, staying out of the way. Sometimes he says something in Spanish, and my mom answers him. She speaks enough Spanish to get around on vacation, she always said, but it sounds like she knows more than she admits. Then Bob starts to ask my mom a question and she answers him before he even finishes, like their brains are connected. My mom is a planet that has two moons orbiting around it. First one is closer, then the other. *If my father and my stepfather are moons, what am I?* I wonder.

"There you are," Francisco says to me, coming out of the kitchen. "I have been told to relax. Is this where you relax?" He points at the sofa. I nod, and he makes his way there. He pats the spot beside him. "Come, my dear."

I sit next to him. The clock on the wall ticks. I want to pinch myself. Am I really sitting next to my father? It's funny. I never thought about him much, never really wanted to know. I had my mom and I thought that was all I needed. But now I feel like a piece of me—a piece I didn't even know was missing—is now in place. He sighs. It doesn't seem to bother him that we aren't talking. And then I think of something.

"Um," I say. "I found this. I mean, I took this from your desk." I pull the yellowed scrap of paper from my pocket. "I stole it. Just like your book. I'm sorry." I can't take the guilt anymore.

He reaches out and touches the paper but doesn't look at it, doesn't read it. He knows what it is. He closes his eyes and recites, *"Las estrellas no son la misma cosa para todos."*

"What does that mean?"

"It's from a book. *The Little Prince.*"

"I know that book! Just a minute." I run to my room. The bed is unmade, like I left it. My pajamas are still in a messy pile next to the laundry basket. And my book is on my nightstand.

"It's my favorite," I say when I return to the couch.

He takes the worn copy from my hands and holds it like it's something delicate, like a flower. Or maybe something dangerous, like a bomb. *"The stars are different to different people. That's what this quote says. It's from the end of the book, before the sad ending."*

"You must like this book, too? Like my mom does?"

"I do, Matilde, I do. My sister, Mechi, copied these words for me before I went to college in Minnesota. And your mom and I used to read the book together. I've had this a long, long time." He hands me back the paper I stole from him. "I know these words by heart. You keep them." A gift.

I tuck it into the pages of my copy of the book and hug it close.

"The author, you know, was a pilot. He was an expert at finding his way. But it's funny," Francisco says, "that his most famous book is about a pilot who gets lost. And that's how he finds what he's looking for."

I don't say anything. I'm not sure I understand what he's saying. But I know that I love this book and that he loves this book. And a big balloon rises in my chest. A feeling like something big growing, something light and airy and perfect and beautiful. We love something the same. Me and my father.

My mom appears with a platter of hot dogs and vegetarian dogs in her hands, the meat (and fake meat) smelling salty and pleasantly burnt. "Lunch is ready. Mattie, will you tell Mercedes?" I wipe my eyes and nod. "Lucas! Kenny!" she shouts.

"Mercedes!" I call. I lost track of Mercedes while I was talking to Francisco. I set my book on the coffee table and then check the bathroom. Not there. She must be outside. I head to the door. The only thing in front is Francisco's little green car in the driveway. No Mercedes.

"Mercedes!" I yell. "Mercedes!"

I unlatch the gate and head to the backyard. No Mercedes.

"Does Mercedes want lemonade?" my mom calls from the kitchen window.

I shake my head.

"Water?"

"She's not here."

"Who's not where?" She comes out the back door with two glasses of lemonade in her hands. The ice cracks, making a tinkling sound.

"I can't find Mercedes."

"What?"

I follow my mom into the dining room where Lucas, Kenny, Bob, and Francisco are already eating hot dogs. After all my life of just me and my mom, it's strange to see these men and boys at our table. Francisco looks up from his food. "Please, sit." He stands to make room.

"She's not here," I say, shaking my head. "Mercedes isn't here."

"Where is she?" Francisco's anxious face makes me wish for one second that I was the one who was missing. That I was the one our father was worried about. That I was the one who ran away.

Because I'm certain she has. I saw her fists. I knew she was angry. Why didn't I stay with her? Why didn't I grab her and keep her here?

"She ran away," I say.

Those three words are like magic. The house becomes chaos—a swirling, rocking, confused chaos. They call her mom again. Leave another message. They call Cristina. Discuss whether they should call the police. Hug the boys, tell them they better not ever even think about running away. They ask me where she could have gone. As if I know. As if I would know what Mercedes would do. I barely know her. We may be sisters—half sisters—but we've only known each other for a few weeks. I know nothing about her.

All I know is that she has a brother. She knows how to use a flat iron. She misses her mom, even though she doesn't admit it. She likes her nanny, even though she won't admit that, either. She's a good student because school is easy for her.

She's adventurous. She's kind, but only in secret. She loves cross-country running. She wanted to find her dad because she thought it would change everything. I remember Mercedes telling me about Francisco Gómez that day at Laurel Park.

Laurel Park.

My mom and Bob are deep in discussion at the dining room table, which is still cluttered with dirty dishes and half-eaten hot dogs. Kenny is distracting Lucas with a video on the iPad. Francisco is pacing back and forth in the living room. Before any of them can stop me, I slip out the front door.

CHAPTER 44

Mercedes

M y chest pounds and my legs burn. When I reach the swing set, I fling myself onto the grass. The sun scorches my eyes and I squeeze them shut. I want to shout. Yell. Scream. I open one eye. Laurel Park is empty except for a squirrel running up the live oak. So I yell.

"Ahhhhh!" It feels so good, I do it again. "Ahhhh!"

I remember once, when I was four, I stole a pack of bubble gum from the candy aisle at the grocery store after Mom wouldn't buy it for me. When I climbed into the car, I opened the pack and popped a piece in my mouth. She looked at me in the rearview mirror. "What are you eating?" she asked.

"Not eating. Chewing gum," I said with a grin.

"Where did that come from?" I held out the pack of gum. "Did you steal bubble gum?" I nodded. She pulled the car to a stop on the side of the road and got out. She snatched the gum away and told me stealing was wrong. But I remember being confused. I wanted the bubble gum and she had taken it away. I started crying and screaming. That made her more mad. The two of us had temper tantrums on the side of the road. That's how it usually goes with Mom; I get her attention but never in the right way.

Now I can have bubble gum whenever I want. In fact, I get most things I want, almost as soon as I want them. But I'm still angry. Because those aren't the things that I want. They're just things. I want to feel whole. I want to fill up whatever is missing in me.

"Stop!" someone is calling out. "Stop! What's the matter?"

How humiliating. I sit up and wipe my face with the backs of my hands. Who caught me behaving like a baby?

"There you are!"

It's Mattie. She's bending at the waist, hands on her thighs like she can barely stand up. Her face is red and damp with sweat.

"You're out of shape," I say. But I smile because I'm so glad to see her.

"I was worried!" she pants.

"Huh," I grunt. "Was anyone else worried?"

"Francisco was ready to call the police."

Mattie tells me how anxious the adults are, that they called Mom again. *Great*, I think, *I'll get Mom's attention but in the wrong way*. Again. Mattie says we have to let them know where we are. "We could call them, but your phone is at the bottom of the pool at Northern Madrone and mine is still in my locker at school." She holds out her pink-fingernailed hand and pulls me up.

I think about how mean I was to her that first time we came here. How mean I was to her at school. She acted different, talked different. She has odd Minnesota habits and a funny way of talking. Her clothes and her hair. They make her easy to make fun of. Now we're both still wearing the same clothes we wore yesterday. She has a spot of whipped cream on her T-shirt. My own shirt has a splotch of ketchup. Her hair is pulled into a ponytail, but little wisps of frizz escape around her face. Mine is in a similar style, held back with one of *her* hair ties. Without my daily flat iron, I must look as wild as she does. Maybe we're not that different.

"How did you know I would be here?"

We both watch a little boy on a red tricycle lead his father along the sidewalk toward the slide.

"I just knew." Mattie takes a few steps closer to me. "Probably because we're related."

I look at her. And then I do this thing that even I can't believe I'm doing. I relax my fists, take a step, and hug Matilde.

CHAPTER 45

Mattie

can't believe Mercedes is letting me hug her—in public. "Now what?" she asks, pulling away. I pretend I don't notice her wiping tears from her cheeks. "You're the one with the plans."

"We should go back to my house."

"Am I in trouble?"

I shake my head. "I'm not sure that a side trip to the park is going to make much of a difference after we ran away and stayed at the college overnight."

And then we laugh. Because what else can we do?

"Come on," I say. "And no running this time."

She smirks. "You really need to get some exercise, Mattie."

The two of us walk toward my house. Down the hill, across the street, around the corner. I can smell the ocean in the breeze that pulls at my ponytail. Even though it's different from the scent of Minnesota leaves crunching under my feet or wet pavement in September rain, it's not terrible.

"I still can't believe that we did it." I stop and pick up a yellow flower that's fallen on the sidewalk from a blooming tree.

"We got away with it too—almost." Mercedes winks, and I stick the flower behind her ear.

"We accomplished what we set out to do. We found our father."

Mercedes doesn't say anything, but she smiles. Just half a smile, but a smile just the same.

When we reach my block, we pause across the street from the driveway. It's like there's a force field preventing us from going home. Like we're in our own spaceship, hovering among the stars, not quite ready to head back to earth.

"You're lucky," Mercedes says, breaking the silence. "It's a nice house." We both stare at my house. My California, step-family house.

"But your house is gorgeous," I protest. "This one is . . . well, small. For five of us."

"But you have your family."

I picture my mom making snacks for me and Lucas and Kenny after school, driving me to the store for school supplies, helping me bake zucchini bread. She'll find a job eventually and then she won't be around to do these mom things as much, but she would never be gone as much as Mercedes's mom is gone. She would never leave me or the boys with a full-time nanny. My heart squeezes with the thought of what Mercedes is missing.

"You know, you can hang out at my house as much as you want," I say. "You and your brother. Who knows? Maybe Tristan and Lucas will become best friends. We're your family, too."

She doesn't look at me at first. And then, after a long silence, she says, "Cool."

"Mattie!" someone yells. "Mercedes!"

Mom and Bob barrel through the red front door. "They're here!" Bob yells into the house.

Francisco Gómez trips on the step as he rushes outside. I wonder if the little girls dressed in white from the picture on his phone ever run away. His eyebrows are scrunched but his mouth is slowly stretching into a smile. "Thank goodness! Qué alivio," he says in his Colombian voice that's both strange and familiar. "Mercedes! Matilde! Hijitas!" And we run across the street toward him. Toward everyone.

Lucas appears from around the back of the house and hurtles toward us. "Mattie!" He crashes into my arms and hugs me. It's funny—I thought I had lost everything when I left Minnesota, but looking around, I can see how much I've gained. A half sister, a dad, a stepfather, and even a wild little stepbrother. I squeeze him back. And then he yells, "Basketball!"

The adults gathered around us laugh as he makes a beeline toward a ball forgotten under a purple-flowering shrub.

"Oh, you two," my mom says, the air rushing out of her as if she's been holding her breath. "Come in. And, Bob," she says over her shoulder, "lock the front door so these girls don't escape again." Bob chuckles his stepdad-like laugh. "I'm only kind of kidding," my mom says sternly.

Like a parade, we all march inside again. Kenny is sitting on the floor in front of the coffee table, where he's almost done setting up the chess pieces. He's not about to hug me like Lucas did, but he watches as I plop next to him. I move my bishop and he breaks into a grin. Mercedes and Francisco squeeze onto the couch with my mom. Lucas bombards Bob.

Pretty soon everyone—except Kenny—is talking at once. My mom tells Mercedes that she spoke with her mom. Mercedes shrugs as my mom tells her that Jennifer isn't coming back early from Taiwan or wherever she is. My mom's voice has a sharp edge in it. Later, much later, I overhear her telling Bob that she can't imagine not rushing straight home if *her* daughter ran away.

"That's okay," Mercedes says.

"Oh, honey," my mom says, and reaches an arm around Mercedes. She squeezes her in a sideways hug. "You're welcome with us anytime, okay? You two are sisters." My mom reaches down and squeezes my shoulder with the other arm. "Sisters. How lucky you are."

Mercedes and I exchange glances. I brace myself for her to jerk away from my mom's embrace. But Mercedes smiles at me and I smile back. The thread between us is taut and pulls at my heart.

"*Half* sisters," we say. In unison.

CHAPTER 46

Mercedes

I have an idea," Mattie says. We're in my room, finishing our myth diorama. Working on our project is the only fun thing we're allowed to do—if you can call working on homework fun.

After the love fest at Mattie's house, reality set in. Even though Mom wasn't coming home early, she told me that I had to face the consequences of my actions. Our moms decided that we should write apology letters to our teachers and to Northern Madrone College. Even to Darryl the security guard. We were grounded. (Mattie's mom decided to ground her, too, although she had never had that kind of punishment before.) Mom said I couldn't get a new phone until I learned my lesson. (I know that will last about four days when she realizes she can't call me to ask about Tristan.) No outings, no mall, no friends, and absolutely no sleepovers for two weeks. (That probably didn't make much of a difference in Mattie's life.) I guess we should be glad we weren't banished to the sky like that Greek goddess.

"But our myth project is due on Tuesday!" Mattie complained to her mom. "We have to work on it."

And so there's an exception to the punishment: Mattie and Mercedes can still get together to work on their homework.

"Under supervision," Mattie's mom said sternly. But I could see a smile in her eyes.

"My idea is to use Francisco Gómez's story," Mattie suggests, gluing foil stars inside an old shoebox that I painted black. "We can use the same diorama but tell the story of Tima and Yuí. Mrs. Ellingham doesn't need one more project on some old Greek myth. Let's tell one of *our* stories." She pulls *The Seed Sower* out of her backpack.

"You keep this," Frank had said to us before he drove back to Northern Madrone. He handed his book to me. "These are your stories. You are both half Colombian. Descended from South American people—Indigenous people, African slaves, Spanish invaders. The stories of Colombia are your stories, even if you don't know them yet."

Mattie and I shifted and squirmed as we stood in front of him. This felt awkward and momentous at the same time.

"You are my daughters," he said. He had a tear in each eye. "Your mothers come first. They are your world. But I hope to be in your orbit somehow. I missed out on so much. And I might miss out on more. But I'm so happy that you both have so many people who love you. I will be going back into the jungle in December to do more research."

"What if you don't get that grant?" Mattie asked.

He shook his head. "Even without the grant, I must go back. Telling and preserving stories is my calling. That's the way my needle points." He put a hand on his chest as if the compass were next to his heart. "Learning about the lives of others and ourselves. It's how we learn to be better humans. Through stories."

I remembered Mrs. Ellingham saying something similar when we started our mythology project. *Studying the stories of ancient civilizations helps us understand our own lives,* she had said.

"Read these stories, hijas. Learn these stories."

"What about the librarian? Are we going to get into trouble?" Mattie asked.

Frank laughed. "I'll take care of Patricia Piper," he said. "But no more stealing, okay?"

We shook our heads.

"And no more running away, okay?"

We nodded.

"We'll figure out a way for us to keep in touch," he said.

Then we all looked at each other awkwardly. The book was so heavy in my arms—how did Mattie lug it around with her all day? I held it out and let the book fall open to the last page. "The Sky Has Many Secrets." Mattie came in close and I passed the book to her. Together we reread the lines of poetry. He studied the page, too.

"I wrote this poem long ago." His voice was gruff. "After I found out about you, Mattie. And you, Mercedes. About my two daughters. I knew I might never meet you. But I always wanted to."

He sniffled. I was kind of embarrassed for him—a grown man crying. Again.

"Que nostalgia. This poem is my story," our dad said. "It is our story."

CHAPTER 47

Mattie

O n Monday, when we return to school after our adventure at Northern Madrone College, the gossip about what happened has already spread like a California wildfire. Over the weekend, while Mercedes and I put the finishing touches on our mythology project, seventh graders texted each other. They told one other we were kidnapped, that we ran away to San Francisco to catch a boat to South America. At soccer practices and dance classes, they said we were arrested for trespassing, that we fell off a cliff and died. After all the swirling rumors, our class thinks the news that Mercedes and I are half sisters and that our dad works at the college was pretty boring. I guess it just seemed obvious to everyone—we look alike, after all.

The most exciting part for the gossip-hungry seventh graders is that Mrs. Leeds is assigning us after-school detention for a week. I've never had detention before. She also makes us hand deliver our apology letters to our teachers first thing Monday morning. Ms. Garcia purses her lips while she reads our letter. She holds it between her fingers like it has cooties. She's wearing a green-and-pink plaid skirt with a pink T-shirt.

"Get to class," is all she says. She's still my least favorite teacher.

After detention on Monday, the first thing I do when I get home is run to my room and plug in my very dead phone. I can't believe I went a whole weekend without it. When it beeps back to life, I see three messages from Mai.

Guess what?!? I'm coming to California for winter break!!! Are you there?????

My auntie is bringing me and she says I can stay with you for a couple nights if it's ok with your mom and it better be ok and answer me now Mat!

I'm jumping up and down even before I finish reading all three messages. "Mom!" I shout. "Mai is coming at Christmas!"

I don't wait for my mom to answer. I immediately FaceTime Mai. All I can see when she answers is an up-close view of her mouth screaming.

"What took you so long?" she shouts.

I resume jumping up and down. "I haven't had my phone since Friday. You'll never believe everything that happened, Mai!"

Mai pulls back so I can see her whole face. "Something good?"

I think about Francisco and Mercedes and Northern Madrone and Lucas and Kenny and Bob. "Yeah," I say. "Good stuff happened."

"Okay, you have to tell me all about it, but first of all—can you believe I get to come to California? Is your mom cool with me staying with you?"

It will be, I know. And that means that Mai will get to meet Mercedes. My dad will be back in Colombia by then, but she'll get to see my new house and Laurel Park and the Boardwalk.

We'll take Lucas for ice cream, and I'll invite Sunny over for a chess tournament with Kenny. Maybe Mai will have some tips for being an older sister. Or maybe I'm going to be just fine figuring it out on my own.

On Tuesday morning in social studies class, Mercedes waves to me as she walks in carrying the diorama in a big paper shopping bag. I'm nervous and excited and a little bit sick. Even before Mercedes gets to her seat, Mrs. Ellingham clears her throat and announces the rules for watching mythology presentations. And then she checks her clipboard and says, "Mattie Gómez and Mercedes Miller will be presenting first."

I feel myself turn red from my toes to my ears. I hate being first at anything. But Mercedes beams like she just won the lottery.

"We'll need to turn the lights off for our presentation, Mrs. Ellingham," she says, setting our diorama on the table at the front of the room.

November jumps up and switches off the lights. The class erupts in obnoxious noise, just like they did when it went dark in the planetarium.

"Silence, class," Mrs. Ellingham scolds. "These two are going to present the Selene myth."

That's what you think, I want to say as I switch on the first set of fairy lightbulbs that poke through the top of the cardboard box. They twinkle like the first stars. The whole class oohs and ahhs. I can't help but smile in the dark. It *is* pretty cool. The diorama shows the silhouette of a mountain range, a blue sea painted on one side. I'm proud of my artwork—I shaded the mountains with purple and turquoise and added white waves to the water. Little plastic trees we found in Tristan's toy box dot the landscape.

"Once upon a time," Mercedes begins.

She introduces Yuí and Tima and their mother. Their cave. I switch the next set of lights on that glow from inside a cave Mercedes made of crumpled paper and tape.

"Yuí flew into the sky and became the sun," Mercedes says, her voice clear and bright. I pull the lever we notched into the cardboard and make the cardboard sun appear. One bright lightbulb shines on it like a spotlight. I hope everyone can see the faint outline of Yuí's face I painted on the yellow disc.

Mercedes continues the story. "The people threw ashes on Tima's face to keep her from escaping." I switch off all the lights for an instant. The whole room is silent, waiting to find out what happens next. What happens to Tima. This is my favorite part of the story. When something bad turns into something good.

Mercedes continues. "But even the ashes on her face couldn't keep her from shining. She followed her brother into the sky. And became the moon." I switch the lights back on and pull the cardboard lever for the moon. "And now the moon and the sun watch over the people of the Sierra Nevada de Santa Marta."

Our classmates applaud. November whoops. I feel all the way proud now. Mercedes is smiling. She doesn't look embarrassed to be seen with me. She looks proud, too.

But then Mrs. Ellingham clears her throat. "This is lovely, girls, but it isn't a myth I've ever heard of. You were supposed to do a Greek myth. You chose Selene. Did you make up this story? You can't just make up a myth. That's not how it works."

"Mrs. Ellingham," I say, trying to keep my voice from shaking. "The story of Tima and Yuí is a myth from the Arhuaco people. The Arhuaco are, um, Native Americans, in Colombia. In South America. We didn't make it up. Honest. We learned about it in this book. This book written by a famous Colombian archaeologist—"

"Anthropologist," Mercedes interrupts. I'll never get that straight. "A famous Colombian anthropologist named Francisco Gómez Flores. He's our dad."

My heart has slowed down to a normal pace. I'm so grateful that Mercedes has taken over. "Show her the book, Mattie," she says.

I head back to my seat by way of the light switch. When the lights flicker back on, everyone groans. I pull *The Seed Sower* out of my backpack and bring it to Mrs. Ellingham.

"It's a real myth. It's just not Greek, not one you've probably heard before," I tell her as she admires the shiny black cover, finds the hidden animals and shapes. "It's important to learn stories from everywhere." I point out the Tima and Yuí story in the book, the book written by our father. "Sometimes," I tell our teacher, "the stories you've never heard before are the most interesting. The ones that can change your life."

CHAPTER 48

Mercedes

M attie!" I call as she heads for her bus after school. Now that it's late October, the cold weather has brought rain and she's wearing her noisy orange jacket. The only good thing about it is that it hides her red sweatshirt with a picture of a grinning hippo on the front. She turns around. "Can you sneak away?" I ask.

Mattie smiles. "I've had some practice."

"Do you want to come to the Boardwalk with us? Cristina is driving."

Mattie hesitates for a moment. Is she going to be too worried about what her mom will say, about what my friends will do, about what might happen? Will she be too anxious about this change in plans? But then she says, "I'll text my mom. I'm sure it'll be fine."

When Cristina pulls up, Mattie climbs into the car behind me and Gaby and Rebecca. Like they always do, my friends ask Cristina to play their favorite songs. They don't say much to Mattie, but I can tell they don't mind having her tag along, either. Gaby and Rebecca totally get that I want to hang out with her sometimes. They aren't about to be best friends with her, but that's fine, because she's become really good friends with Sunny Li. It turns out they both play chess.

"I don't really like rides," Mattie says when Gaby and Rebecca talk about the Tornado Drop, a super-scary one that hauls you up about a million feet and drops you like a stone. "Especially since my stepbrother puked on me after going on one," she adds with an embarrassed giggle.

Rebecca looks at me and I can't help laughing. "Gross!" she says. "We know."

"You what?" Mattie says.

"Don't listen to her," I say.

Gaby laughs. "Mercedes hates rides, too."

I stare at her. "What? Who says?"

"We can tell, Mercedes," Rebecca says. "It's fine." And I wonder about what people know about you even if you don't tell them.

When we get to the Boardwalk, Cristina drops us off by the arcade. "It gets dark by six thirty, so don't be late," she says before she drives away.

"Let's go see if Joaquin is here!" Gaby shrieks. Mattie and I follow her and Rebecca to the arcade, where they crowd around Joaquin and the other boys. I play Super Dance Shuffle. Mattie tries it, too, but she's not as good as me.

Then we play air hockey, and she beats all the boys.

"Must be my Minnesota blood," she says and high-fives me.

"Roller coaster time!" shouts Rebecca.

"You guys go on," I say. "Unless you want to?" I wink at Mattie.

Instead, we go in search of cotton candy. It turns out to

be one of the things we have in common. The Boardwalk will close for winter soon and some of the booths are already shuttered, but we find a stand. Blue for her, pink for me.

"Let's go on the beach," I suggest. Gaby and Rebecca never want to leave the games and rides. Sometimes I like a little break from the noise and lights.

We shove mouthfuls of cotton candy in our mouths and trudge across the cold, damp sand to the shore. "It's like walking through snow," Mattie says. "Except, well, sandier."

"Do you miss snow?"

"No, not as much as I thought I would. I like this kind of weather—cool, a little cloudy, a little rain."

"I love this weather, too." I run ahead. "Come on." I dash out in the wet sand, then run back to avoid the waves. It's my favorite game. Keep Away, Tristan calls it.

Mattie and I run forward and then backward, shrieking when a wave gets a little too close. I drop my cotton candy in the sand and a gull tries to snatch it. Mattie and I laugh. We spin in circles until we're dizzy, and I remember the two of us balancing in our dad's hammock, swinging back and forth, trying to position ourselves just right so we didn't fall off. Behind us, the neon lights of the Boardwalk switch on, brilliant against the darkening sky.

"Watch out!" Mattie yells, but it's too late. My brand-new, lime-green sneaker is soaked with icy water. I scream from the cold and shock and run up the beach. I collapse on dry sand like a wounded soldier, but instead of dying, I'm laughing. "Your new shoes," Mattie says, plopping down beside me.

"They'll dry," I say. "But, wow, is that cold!"

We sit on the damp sand and I take off my shoe, squeeze out my sock. I balance my bare foot on Mattie's knee. I wiggle my lime-green toenails. Around us, a chilly wind blows off the water. Her jacket makes a loud rustling noise as she zips it to her chin. The faint light of the moon peeks out from behind a cloud.

"My mom is coming home in a couple weeks," I say. "She wants to invite Frank to Thanksgiving. Before he goes back to Colombia. Your family is invited, too."

"That'll be weird," she says. I nod. We haven't seen much of Frank Gómez. He took us hiking one weekend, which was nice. We talked about visiting him someday. But for now, he's already packing his office and getting ready to return to the jungle. I think about his compass, the one that points him away from us. I wonder where mine will point.

"Look," Mattie says. "First star."

I stretch out on my back. I gaze at the light twinkling above us. Venus? Mars? If we hadn't skipped the planetarium, I'd probably know.

"If you stare at a dark spot long enough," she says, "you'll notice another star. Every time I think there's nothing there, another star appears."

We lie on the beach and watch as more stars pop out one by one.

"Isn't that Cassiopeia?" I ask.

Mattie's eyes follow the direction I'm pointing. "Yep."

"When I first learned about Cassiopeia," I say, thinking of that night camping with Mom and Tristan and his dad, "I was so mad when Tristan's dad told me that it's known as the W constellation. I thought it was an *M*." I arc my arm, making a huge *M* across the sky. "You know, for Mercedes."

"Let's pretend it is. *M* for Mercedes and *M* for Mattie."

I smile in the dim glow from the Boardwalk. "That's what Tristan's dad said."

"He sounds nice."

An M *for Mercedes.* "He is."

Mattie continues, almost to herself, "My stepdad is pretty nice, too."

I look up at Cassiopeia again. "Technically, Tristan's dad isn't my stepdad." I pause. "But maybe it doesn't matter."

"It doesn't," Mattie says confidently. "Who cares what anyone is *technically*? I mean, I have this whole new family who's not even related to me."

I nod. She's right, I suppose. I think about how Tristan's dad isn't mine, but he's still part of my family. Sometimes even more than Mom. And Tristan is still my favorite little brother ever.

"You know what?" Mattie says. "I'm not going to tell anyone you're my half sister anymore.

My head snaps to stare at her. What? Is she embarrassed of me now? My shoulders tense and my hands curl into fists.

She grins as widely as the hippo on her sweatshirt. "I'm going to call you my *sister*."

And my hands relax. My shoulders release. I look over at Mattie. My sister. We lock eyes for a moment. Our matching pairs, eyes that look a lot like Frank Gómez's eyes.

"You're a dork, Matilde."

And we both collapse into giggles, hysterical. We laugh

until we can't laugh anymore. When our laughter dies down, we can hear the whistling sound of the wind as it skims the water. The screams from the roller coaster and the tinny music from the arcade float across the sand. My sister and I catch our breath and study the sky, all those stars.

"It's funny," Mattie says after a moment, "the sky here is the same as the sky in Minnesota. When I look up, I feel like I'm home."

She can't see me in the dark, but I nod.

"I think the sky is like a book," I say. She doesn't say anything, but I know Mattie agrees. "You open the book, and the pages in front of you could take you anywhere. Endless possibilities."

She sighs. "It's like a story that's just beginning."

ACKNOWLEDGMENTS

As with all books, this one couldn't have happened without many supportive people. Thank you first to my agent, Thao Le, and my editor, Amanda Ramirez, for letting me write another sibling story.

When I was twenty-five, I found out that I had a half brother, one of the best surprises of my life. While it was confusing and difficult at times, that meeting inspired this story. Special thanks to him for being part of my life (and giving me a beautiful nephew and niece).

Thank you to my dad, who gave me his well-loved copy of *The Little Prince* and has always known which way his compass points. And thank you to his wife for her help in tracking down the mythology of Indigenous Colombian cultures like the Arhuaco. Any errors in the storytelling or translations are mine alone.

This book is dedicated to my mom, who introduced me to the Hayley Mills version of *The Parent Trap* and who read aloud E. L. Konigsburg's *From the Mixed-Up Files of Mrs. Basil E. Frankweiler*, both of which inspired Mattie and Mercedes's adventure.

As always, I am indebted to my family. To Sylvia, who helped brainstorm plot points and picked out Mercedes's outfits. To Dave, who supports me in all ways a writer needs to be supported.